On Her Doorstep

Also by Kay Hooper
in Large Print:

Stealing Shadows
Elusive Dawn
Eye of the Beholder
After Caroline
It Takes a Thief
Rafe, the Maverick
Return Engagement

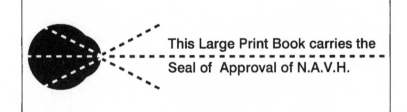

On Her Doorstep

KAY HOOPER

Thorndike Press • Thorndike, Maine

Published in 2001 by arrangement with The Berkley Publishing Group, a member of Penguin Putnam Inc.

Thorndike Press Large Print Romance Series.

The tree indicium is a trademark of Thorndike Press.

The text of this Large Print edition is unabridged.
Other aspects of the book may vary from the original edition.

Set in 16 pt. Plantin by Minnie B. Raven.

Printed in the United States on permanent paper.

Library of Congress Cataloging-in-Publication Data

Hooper, Kay.
   On her doorstep / Kay Hooper.
     p. cm.
   ISBN 0-7862-3192-0 (lg. print : hc : alk. paper)
   1. Large type books.   I. Title.
   PS3558.O587 O5   2001
   813'.54—dc21   00-067300

For my sister, Linda.
In celebration of her second chance.

Chapter One

It wasn't a real body, of course.

Or, rather, Erin thought decidedly, not a *dead* body; it looked real enough, but it was breathing. She shifted her weight onto her other foot and studied the breathing body thoughtfully.

"It's alive, Chester," she said.

Chester sat down in the dirt and sighed heavily, his bloodshot eyes peering at the body with the unfocused and wholly disinterested look of an alcoholic after a weekend binge. Which was the case.

Erin could sympathize with her companion, but, unlike Chester, her own lack of focus came from a horrendous case of jet lag. Call it jet lag, anyway. Or just plain exhaustion. She felt light-headed, and her body was slow to obey the commands of her brain — which was performing at something less than the norm.

"Hey!" She nudged the breathing body with one boot rudely.

The body stirred, said something hardly polite, and subsided again.

Erin looked down at Chester and said, "Bite him."

"If he does, I'll shoot him," said the body.

Since Chester showed no disposition to bite anything at all, this threat wasn't put to the test.

"You're on my porch," Erin told the body coldly.

The body stirred again. A sunbrowned hand reached up to push back a western hat, revealing a lean face stubbled with beard from which a pair of bloodshot gray eyes peered at her unhappily.

Erin repeated her statement even more coldly. "You're on my porch."

"This place is empty," he disagreed in a deep, weary voice.

"Only because I wasn't here. I am now. So it isn't empty. Go away."

He folded his tall length into a sitting position, removed the hat to run fingers through Indian-straight raven hair, replaced the hat firmly but in an oddly unpracticed gesture, and squared his broad shoulders as if he were prepared — now — to deal with the situation.

He peered past her to see two horses, one a pack horse heavily laden with unidentifiable packages covered with canvas. He sighed and swung his boots off the porch, getting to his feet reluctantly. "Well," he said, "since you live here — apparently — maybe you can tell me where to locate someone. I've been looking for two days. They said in town it was a cabin, and this is the only one I found."

"I know nothing about my neighbors." She was slightly annoyed to find that he was bigger standing than he'd looked lying down.

He regarded her for a moment, then shifted his gaze to Chester's depressed form. "What in God's name is that?"

Chester lifted a lip at him.

"That," Erin said coldly, "is my dog."

The man appeared somewhat bemused by Chester. "Somebody's pulling your leg, lady. That's not a dog, it's a mutant grizzly."

Erin felt offended on Chester's behalf, but could hardly cavil at the apt description. Her dog did rather resemble a grizzly, especially since his head (no doubt painful) was hanging low so that he looked as if he had a humped back. In addition, he was very large and muscular, with a dense coat of grayish-brown hair. And when he yawned — as he did at that moment — he displayed a set of pearly whites that any grizzly would have claimed with pride.

Deciding to ignore the insult to her pet,

Erin stared at the man and felt a vague curiosity. "How did you get up here?" She looked him up and down while he seemed to consider his answer, adding, "You look like you walked."

He glanced briefly down at himself, at the jeans and flannel shirt liberally coated with dust, then stared at her. Ignoring her question, he said politely, "Mind telling me what a delicate little creature like you is doing out here in the back of beyond?"

Since the three-inch heels of Erin's boots put her at exactly six feet, and since she was what men tended to term "voluptuous," this was clearly sarcasm of the first order. Looking up at him (something she didn't often have to do), she said sweetly, "I needed peace and quiet for my knitting."

A grin tugged at his mouth, but gave up the struggle. "They tell me there are real bears up here, you know," he offered with a glance down at Chester.

Erin wondered who had told him. "Good," she said dryly. "I could use a new rug."

He clearly decided she was kidding. "I wouldn't think it would be safe here," he pursued gravely. "And not just because of the bears. I've heard the weather up here gets wild this time of year; you could be completely cut off. There's no power here, and that old generator in the shed hasn't worked in years from the looks of it. You'd be better off —" He stopped, since she'd turned and gone to her horse. A moment later she was before him again, and he took an involuntary step back.

Erin slid two shells into the shotgun and closed the breech with a quietly deadly snap. She held the gun negligently, the barrel pointed at his belt buckle. "You were saying?"

"I'll just get my horse," he murmured, eyeing the shotgun.

"Do that." She waited calmly.

He disappeared around the corner of the log cabin, returning a few moments later atop a roan horse with a rather wicked eye. A familiar horse. Erin took due note of the horse's unpredictable nature. She also took note of the man's obvious unfamiliarity with horses in general and this one in particular. One never knew, after all, when such information would come in handy.

And it did. Rather quickly.

"Look, lady," he said, trying again, "I'm just looking for someone in this Godforsaken place. J. D. Mathers. And I'd appreciate it if you —"

Smoothly, Erin raised the shotgun and

11

fired both barrels into the air. The roan, as she'd expected, bolted. She listened to blue curses growing fainter as angry hooves carried horse and rider away, then she sighed and looked down at Chester.

Head hanging, front legs splayed, he had both eyes closed and was whimpering softly. Opening first one eye and then the other, he gave Erin a look of heartrending reproach.

"Sorry, Chester. I forgot."

He lifted a lip at her. There was no malice in the gesture; it was just Chester's way of remarking. "The hell you say." Wearing the mien of a dog to whom torture was a daily thing, he staggered onto the porch and collapsed with a groan.

Absently, Erin ejected the spent shells and leaned the shotgun up against the wall near her dog. She paused a moment to adjust her hat, pushing a stray lock of hair underneath it. Then, sighing, she went to begin unloading her things.

She was so tired that her mind was in a fog, but a faint glimmer of sheepish guilt rose when she realized just how badly she'd behaved to what had been, after all, a harmless stranger. Carrying loads of gear from horses to cabin, she mused about that. But she was too tired to accept the guilt.

He'd been on her porch, after all. *Her*

porch. Without so much as a "Pardon me, lady, but may I take a nap on your porch?" He'd just *been* there. Six feet and a few odd inches of blue-jeaned, booted, dust-coated, beard-stubbled man lying on her porch.

Erin began to feel severely put-upon. She relished the feeling.

And why, she wondered tiredly, was he looking for J. D. Mathers? Nobody ever looked for Mathers. Ever. Mathers was a recluse who had made it abundantly plain to any and all that visitors were, not to put too fine a point on it, unwelcome. Mathers's wishes, generally honored, had become scrupulously honored when a curious reporter had bolted back down the mountain some months before with a load of buckshot in his Calvin Kleins.

Erin, methodically rubbing down her horses in the small but sturdy barn behind the cabin, wondered vaguely if the man on her porch had been told about that. Probably. And, in spite of the dust coating his sturdy clothes, Erin had easily detected the gloss of city beneath.

Only innate grace and an instinctive sense of balance had kept him on the bolting roan; he was no horseman. So what was a city-bred stranger doing up here in the back of beyond?

J. D. Mathers, obviously.

Erin fed her horses and stabled them, then went into the shed to start up the generator. It looked disused, as the stranger had noticed, but worked like a charm after Erin talked to it, kicked it companionably, and made a few other minor adjustments. It choked and sputtered at first, then settled down to a busy roar.

She went into the cabin just in time to save the pack Chester was clawing frantically. Carrying the pack into the kitchen area of the roomy cabin, Erin sent a frown back at her whimpering canine friend. "No. Hair of the dog would kill you in your condition."

Chester whimpered. He grumbled and groaned and growled, complaining at great length.

Erin pulled a half-full bottle of whiskey from the pack and placed it high on a shelf. "You," she told Chester, "are going on the wagon. Get that? You're five years old and a hopeless alcoholic. It's pathetic. No more booze. If I ever see Stuart again, I'll shoot him for both of us."

She hoped she wouldn't see Stuart again. She was no longer bitter after three years, but those years had been spent up here in very rough country and she had a feeling . . .

14

Well, there was neither city gloss nor city manners in her any longer.

If she saw him again, she'd probably kill him.

Erin started laughing as that realization surfaced. It was, curiously, the sound of release. Three years ago she had run with her tail between her legs, bruised and wounded and confused, and now she could contemplate, with detachment, killing the cause of all that distant pain.

Good. She was over him.

Still, it had been lousy of Stuart to turn Chester into an alcoholic. She was very glad now that she had rescued her dog last year. Kidnapped him, really, while Stuart had been gone from the house.

Erin looked longingly at her bedroom, tiredness almost overwhelming her. But she was a tidy person and knew she wouldn't be able to rest until her supplies were put away. Methodically, she stored everything neatly in the shining pine cabinets that she had built herself. She swept the dust of two weeks away until the hardwood floor gleamed dully, then polished tables and shelves and counters.

Somewhere during the tidying, she put on coffee and drank it black while she worked, trying to stay awake until everything was done. Compulsive, she thought. I'm compulsive. Not that it bothered her. She didn't ask anyone but Chester to live with her compulsiveness, and he minded only the whiskey bottle kept out of his reach.

The refrigerator was getting cold, and Erin went to her radio to call down to town. She alerted the grocer with whom she did infrequent business, and Mal promised to send perishables in his battered Jeep; could she meet the delivery at Black Rock? She promised to do so.

"There is," Mal remarked, "a stranger in town. Looking for Mathers."

"He was on my porch," Erin responded. "Did you — ?"

Mal was shocked. " 'Course not, Erin. I'd never. But I don't think he'll give up. Should I — ?"

Erin considered the matter, sighed. "Guess not. The roan'll probably kill him anyway. Tell Jake the guy can't ride, but he sticks a horse like flypaper. Strong legs, I imagine. The roan didn't lose him, anyway."

Mal clucked in disappointment. "Jake thought for sure. I mean, well, he looked like a dude. Came in wearing a three-piece suit, Brooks Brothers written all over it. Bought his jeans and stuff here when he realized

16

he'd have to climb the mountain. Cussed up a storm."

Behind Erin, Chester howled mournfully.

"He's on the wagon again?" Mal asked interestedly.

"Yes," Erin said, "and tell Jake if he slips him whiskey one more time, I'll shoot him. I appreciate him renting the roan to that guy, but I won't have Chester drink anymore. It's starting to affect his health."

"Thought he had a cast-iron stomach."

Erin glanced back at her unhappy dog, then told the radio, "The booze he's swallowed could eat through the hull of a battleship. Especially that stuff Jake makes. Tell him to quit it. Or at least quit giving it to Chester."

"Okay," Mal agreed cheerfully. "You want the same supplies as usual, Erin?"

She mentally went over her standard list, known to both of them, then nodded before remembering she was on the radio. "Same, I guess. A little more cheese this time. And some fresh vegetables. My garden was raided."

"You *will* feed the animals," Mal reminded her dryly. "They get to expect it after a while. Your own fault."

"Mmmm." Erin sighed again. "Signing off, Mal. I've got to sleep."

"Jeep'll be at Black Rock at ten in the morning," Mal said. "As usual. Bye, Erin."

She replied in kind, then turned off her radio and yawned. Leaving the small utility room where she kept the radio, she went into the large living room of the cabin and looked around. Clean and neat, just as she liked it.

She went into the bathroom and turned on the faucet to allow rusty water to escape, waiting for clear. Then she tried the hot and was gratified to find the heater had managed lukewarm. She filled the huge claw-footed tub and dumped in bath salts. Chester came in and began to drink out of the tub; she shoved him out, swearing mildly, closed the door behind him, and undressed, listening to him complain, He had water in the kitchen, but apparently liked the taste of bath salts.

Then she slid into the warm water and relaxed, allowing muscles to ease, dust to be washed away. To avoid falling asleep, she forced herself to sit up and soap a cloth and rub busily to remove stubborn dirt. She used a hand shower attachment to wash her hair, forgetting the pins and having to stop for a moment to remove them.

When she was clean and glowing, she climbed reluctantly from the tub and toweled off briskly. She found her hair dryer and stood before the antique mirror above the gleaming oak vanity, drying her hair, brushing the long mass with soothing strokes.

Clean. Finally! Two weeks of camping had left her feeling decidedly dusty; the stream had been far too cold to bathe in.

Erin turned the dryer off, vaguely aware of Chester making a disinterested comment outside the door. Rummaging in the narrow closet where she kept linens and sleepwear (more convenient, since she always bathed before bed), she located a pair of rather brief black silk pajamas and looked at them doubtfully.

Then, shrugging, she pulled the silk over smooth skin. If she had associated clothing with memories, she might have felt odd to still wear garments Stuart had bought for her; fortunately, Erin didn't care. So she stepped without pain into bottoms that clung lovingly to her curved hips and long legs, then shrugged into the top that was plunging of neckline and also loving. She buttoned the top, reflecting absently that she'd finally gained back the weight shed during those tumultuous first months with Stuart; the black silk gaped just a bit over her full breasts.

Then she opened the door and padded

out into the living room, nearly tripping over Chester, who looked up at her and commented mildly again. She looked up at the front door for a moment, then back at her dog.

"Some watchdog," she told him.

Chester commented again, clearly saying that he *had* tried, after all, but that she hadn't listened. Then, his dogly duty discharged, he went to the cold fireplace, looked at it distrustfully for an instant, and collapsed on the hearth rug with a groan.

Erin returned her gaze to the front door. The open front door. And the dusty stranger leaning against the jamb, who was staring at her in some surprise.

"We-e-ll," he said, the word drawled out. "You certainly look different with your — uh — hair down."

"I thought I sent you away," Erin said.

He smiled, showing strong white teeth and little humor. "I came back."

Sighing, Erin padded around the low partition that divided kitchen from living room, and poured another cup of coffee. Obviously, she had company for a while. With faint irony she lifted her cup questioningly at the stranger.

"Thank you." He accepted politely, straightening away from the jamb and coming to the other side of the partition.

Erin poured another cup, looked at him in inquiry and was told he took it black, then handed him the cup.

"We got off on the wrong foot," he told her after an appreciative sip of coffee. "My name is Matt Gavin, and I'm from New York. From Salem Publishing. I'm looking for J. D. Mathers."

"Whomever you may be looking *for*," she said dryly, "you're looking *at* my pajama top. At, specifically, my bust."

He grinned suddenly, gray eyes that were sheepish lifting to her face. "Sorry," he murmured. "At least — Hell, I'm not sorry. I'm human. And the flannel shirt and jeans you were wearing before didn't even hint — I mean — and your hair, is it —" He stopped suddenly.

"It's real," she told him dryly. "Given my druthers, I wouldn't have chosen red." She paused for a moment, then added gently, "Mr. Gavin, it's difficult to talk to someone who won't look you in the eye."

He seemed to withdraw his gaze with great effort and fixed it on his coffee cup. "Then," he muttered, "button that damned top."

She looked down, swore mildly, and refastened two gaping buttons. "It wasn't

21

intentional," she told him. "I've gained some weight."

"All in the right places." He fumbled in a pocket, finding cigarettes and lighter. "Do you mind — ?" He didn't look at her.

Erin found an ashtray and pushed it across the narrow bar that topped the partition. Then she leaned against the counter behind her, sipping coffee and trying to hide the gap. Useless, she decided, and set her cup aside to go into her bedroom. When she returned, the silk top had been replaced by a loose pullover top.

He looked at her over the partition and sighed. "You haven't told me your name."

"I didn't know it mattered."

"Look —" he began.

Erin lifted a hand, halting him. "Mr. Gavin" — she spoke slowly, as if to someone a bit, just a bit, dense — "I have just returned from two weeks of camping. Eventful camping. I am very, very tired. If I don't get some sleep quite soon, I won't be responsible for my actions. I am in no mood to stand in my cabin and talk to a stranger."

He drew on the cigarette, staring at her. His eyes dropped fleetingly to her now decently covered superstructure and seemed to flicker in momentary sadness. Then, as if it were a throwaway line, he said, "My horse is gone."

Erin blinked. "Threw you, did he." It wasn't a question.

"No. I got off outside and he just — ran away."

"You didn't tie him?"

Matt Gavin smiled sheepishly. She was beginning to mistrust that sheepish smile. It had a motive under it.

"Then," Erin said, "you walk."

"It's ten miles down this mountain."

"Better get started then. It'll be dark in a few hours." Erin would have looked at her watch, except that she didn't own one. It would, she thought, have made her comment more pointed if she could have looked at her watch.

Seeming to ignore her advice, he half-turned to gaze around the neat cabin. A place for everything and everything in its place. Shining floors dotted here and there with bright throw rugs. Comfortable over-stuffed furniture. A lovely rock fireplace with split logs piled handily in the stone wood box beside it. Floor-to-ceiling oak bookshelves on two walls. The third wall formed the front of the cabin and boasted wide windows, curtained lightly in gauzy whiteness; the fourth wall contained the small kitchenette and a short hallway with three doors turning off it.

One door was the bath, the second the bedroom; the third door was firmly closed and announced nothing.

He turned back to her after contemplating that closed door for a long, pointed moment. Then, mildly, he said, "I'll double your next advance if that door doesn't hide your office."

She blinked, stared at him. After a minute of silence, she poured more coffee and sipped. Then she looked at him again and sighed.

"J. D. Mathers, I presume?" His voice was very polite. "Who signs her contracts in the name E. Scott. Which stands for — ?"

"Erin." She sighed again, aware that she was too tired to cope with this invasion. Aware she would have to cope whether she wanted to or not. "Why couldn't you have just gone away?" It was, obviously, a rhetorical question.

He recognized it as such and ignored it.

"What," he asked, "is this mania of yours all about? I mean, granted, you have the right to live alone if you want. But up here? Miles from nothing? You won't talk to us on the phone, you refuse to promote your books — not that they need it — you've refused a dozen invitations to come to New York —"

"Mr. Gavin." Erin was tired, she knew that, and wished she could shut her own mouth before her tiredness led her into areas she really didn't want to tread. "It is, as you said, my right to live as I choose. I choose to live here. Why is none of your business." It was said politely, quietly. Firmly.

He was studying her, his gray eyes nearly as weary as the green ones that looked back at him. But his eyes were sharp nonetheless. He gazed from the shining, incredibly vibrant waist-length copper hair, over the loose-fitting (pity, that, he thought) top, and down to the narrow waist that was all he could see before the partition got in his way.

Then he looked at her face, searching, intent. He found eyes so green that they could have defined the color, and they were framed by long dark lashes. A complexion that was translucent and beautifully pale (no wonder, he thought, she'd worn a hat earlier; she'd burn *very* easily no matter what time of the year). A straight, delicate nose. Lips that were full and curved with innate humor. Stubborn chin.

All in all, he decided, she had a face that men dreamed about, poets wrote about, singers sang about . . . A face that could launch ships. Lovely. Just lovely. Colorado, he thought, was looking better, too. Now that he'd found her in Colorado.

Still, he could see nothing in that lovely face to indicate why she hid herself away up here. It was, he thought, a waste. A *criminal* waste.

Erin, who was perceptive even when tired and had considerable experience in seeing men look at her, watched his lean face change expression and wished, wryly, that the roan had thrown him.

She was, she suspected, stuck with him.

"Mr. Gavin, is there some reason you came up here to find me? I'm just curious, you understand."

With a start he realized he'd forgotten business. He had, he thought, begun to forget business the instant her top had gaped at him. He cleared his throat. "About your next book." When she remained politely unresponsive, he tried again. "We're scheduling, and we need a title. And chapters, if possible. For the artwork. The cover."

She looked around the cabin for a moment, then back at him. "Couldn't you have just written a letter?" Then remembered that he had.

"I did. You didn't answer. And, besides —"
He hesitated, then shrugged. "So damned
reclusive. We wondered. And we've had re-
quests for you to speak, and appear on television —"

"No."

"Your last book," he reminded her, "was
on every major best-seller list for months.
Months. In fact, it's still there. People want
to see you, hear you, know about you. You
won't even release a *picture,* for god-sake."

Erin felt temper creeping, and with it the
realization that she was going to tread where
she didn't want to. The man's persistence
made it inevitable. "Mr. Gavin —"

"Matt."

"Whatever. If you'll reread my contracts,
you'll find that we got rid of the standard
clauses about promoting books. I won't do
that. They can read my books or not, criti-
cize or not, speculate — or not. I don't care.
I don't watch television. I don't like cities.
And I won't promote the books."

"We could sell even more."

"I don't care."

He looked at her, a man who was handsome in spite of the stubble and coating of
dust, a man with a determined jaw. And he
smiled, this time with humor.

"I'll try to convince you, you know."

"I know." She sighed inaudibly. "But you won't succeed. It'll take time for you to realize that, unfortunately. Pity you won't just take my word for it."

He shook his head. Slowly and firmly.

"Uh-huh." Erin looked at him and felt even more tired. "But in the meantime, leave. I have got to get some sleep."

"My horse."

"Take one of mine. The sorrel, not the gray." Remembering whom she was talking to, she added, "The brown one."

Matt Gavin considered the matter. "Look," he said, "we're both tired. And if I have to ride back down this mountain today, I'll get myself killed. You have a couch." He looked, added, "A comfortable couch. Take your shotgun into the bedroom if you don't trust me, but have a heart and let me sleep on your couch."

"No."

He looked at her pathetically. "I'd like children someday. If I have to get back on a horse," he said, "I'll never be able to father children."

It surprised a laugh out of her. She realized, while he gazed at her appealingly, that he was determined to stay. She also realized she was just too damned tired to argue about it.

28

"Oh, hell," she said. "Take the couch. I'm going to bed." She turned toward the hall, then hesitated and crossed to get the shotgun leaning near the door. Pointedly, she reloaded it, then smiled at him gently and retreated to her bedroom.

She was, literally, asleep before her head hit the pillow.

Chapter Two

It had been mid-afternoon when Erin had flopped the covers over her and abandoned the world and the stranger out in her living room; it was, she judged, early morning when she woke. The cabin was silent and still.

She threw back covers and slid from the double bed, going to the window and parting gauzy curtains. She looked for and found the sun rising behind the cabin, nodding to herself. *Early* morning.

It took only a few moments for her to dress in jeans and a bulky sweater, to brush her long thick hair and wrestle it into a ponytail high on her head. In socks and carrying her boots, she padded into the living room and stood gazing down on her stranger.

Either, she thought, he hadn't wanted to dirty her off-white couch with his dusty clothes, or else he simply preferred not to sleep in his clothes. His jeans and flannel shirt were folded with an attempt at neatness and reposed on her square coffee table. As for himself, he was wrapped in the colorful afghan that had graced the back of the couch.

And it covered him decently only by liberal standards.

For a moment she studied him. He was even more beard-stubbled, his lean face relaxed and vulnerable in sleep; dark lashes lay in thick crescents against his cheekbones. His raven hair was tousled, a lock falling over his high forehead.

Broad shoulders rose nakedly from the afghan, tanned and strong (sunlamp? she wondered — he was a city man, after all). A thick mat of black hair covered his chest. One powerful arm lay outside the afghan, and one long leg was bared as well.

She found her eyes fixed on the steadily rising and falling chest, and frowned a little. There was an odd weakness in her knees and her own breathing seemed to quicken. She fought a sudden urge to touch him, her frown deepening.

Ridiculous. She wasn't attracted to this stranger.

Erin slowly turned away, going into the kitchen and setting her boots down to start making coffee. Mid-thirties, she decided. No wedding ring, but that meant little.

Nor did her weak knees mean anything, she decided firmly. Except perhaps that she'd been alone up here for too long.

Erin grimaced as she measured the grounds, ignoring the impulse to turn and stare at him again. He was a *stranger,* and he'd be gone soon.

When the coffee was perking, she quietly retrieved his clothes and took them, along with some of her own, out to the little laundry room by the back door. Chester came in through the pet door as she was starting the washing machine, looking better today but still bad-tempered, judging from the growl with which he greeted her.

Erin followed her pet from the laundry room, closing the door to cut the noise. She went out back to feed and water the horses, then returned to the cabin. She found her guest still sleeping soundly and coffee ready for drinking. She fixed breakfast for Chester but none for herself, leaning against the partition while she drank coffee and stared broodingly at Matt Gavin.

Why couldn't she stop staring at him?

She was on her second cup when she dimly heard the washing machine cut off, and went to transfer clothing into a basket and carry it out to hang on the line behind the cabin. The morning air held a faint chill, but the sun promised a warm day with a soft breeze, and Erin preferred to hang out her clothes whenever possible.

When she returned, Matt Gavin was still asleep.

Erin shrugged to herself, jotted a quick note and left it on the coffee table, then went out to saddle her horse. She took the sorrel, Amos, leaving the gray, Tucker, in his stall munching hay. Specially made saddlebags dangled behind her saddle, large bags that would hold the provisions Mal was sending up.

She mounted at the barn and rode around the cabin, finding Chester sitting on the porch. He looked at her, ears lifting.

"You stay here," she told him, and he lay down with a gusty sigh.

It took nearly an hour to reach Black Rock — which was the nearest to her cabin a wheeled vehicle could manage (and only a four-wheel drive could get that far). A battered black Jeep was parked beside the jutting black rock that had named the spot, and sitting on the hood was a young man engrossed in a book.

"Hi, Jake," Erin called as she reached him.

Spaniel-brown eyes rose to hers, eyes shining with a deceptive innocence and a not-so-deceptive intelligence. "Morning, Erin." He grinned at her. "Mal gave me your message. I promise, no more tea for Chester."

"Tea!" Erin dismounted, shaking her head. "D'you know how I used that jug you sent me? I stripped varnish off an antique rocking chair."

"Yes, it's good for that," Jake agreed, not at all offended by her use of the concoction he fondly called "tea" and which he gleefully sold to amused townspeople to supplement his income. He joined Erin at the rear of the Jeep and began helping her transfer provisions into her saddlebags. "Erin — that guy. Didn't come back to town. The roan did, though, just a little while ago."

"He's on my couch." Erin looked at Jake, shook her head.

Jake gave her a thoughtful look. "Uh-huh. Nice-looking guy," he added casually.

Erin remembered a nearly naked male body on her couch and cleared her throat. "I suppose. But he's a city boy, Jake. He'll get tired of the wilderness soon enough."

Jake sat on the tailgate of the Jeep, still thoughtful. The book he'd been reading was stuck in the back pocket of his jeans, and he pulled it out to gaze at it absently.

Erin looked at the title, not surprised to find that the book dealt with chemical composition. Jake, although heaven knew he didn't look it, was something of a genius.

"Erin . . ." Jake looked up, frowning. "When you first came up here, you were — well, thin, pale, nervy. Like you'd been kicked in the stomach. You were like a ghost at first, slipping into town a few times, then slipping out. Didn't want to be bothered. So we didn't. Then you started talking to Mal, me, a few others. Opened up.

"Now —" He ran impatient fingers through thick brown hair and sighed. "Hell, now you're one of us. And we worry about you. There's nothing wrong with living alone if that's what you like, and you seem to like it. But you're a beautiful woman who's had most of the softness kicked out of you, and that's not good. Maybe . . . maybe you've been up here long enough."

It was, she heard, a reluctant suggestion. And she smiled a little. "What brought that on?"

He grinned faintly. "The dude, I guess. He's the first stranger to get this close since you came. We all guessed there was someone for you once; you've got the kind of scars only a man could put on a woman. And you — I don't think you're a woman who'd want to live alone all her life, Erin."

Erin didn't even think of mocking or scorning his tailgate psychology; he was serious, and he cared about her. So she smiled at him as she mounted her horse.

"Thanks for worrying, Jake. But I've found something up here I've never known before. Call it peace if you like. I'm happy here. So stop worrying. And say hello to Randi for me, okay?"

"Okay. She wanted to come up and visit, but the doctor —"

"You tell her to stay put and take care of herself. I'll come down in a week or so and visit." She kept her voice light; after three years it had gotten easier.

"The baby might be here by then," Jake said, the pride and anxiety of an about-to-be father in his voice. "Randi looks like she's swallowed a basketball."

Erin laughed, waved good-bye, and headed Amos back up the mountain.

When she carried the saddlebags into the cabin more than an hour later, she noted in passing that her guest's jeans and flannel shirt were gone from the line out back. Once in the cabin, she heard the shower going and was not surprised to find the couch bare of an almost-naked stranger.

Chester, who had met her out front and accompanied her through the unsaddling and stabling process, stood and watched hopefully while she unpacked and put away the perishables. When neither labeled whiskey nor Jake's "tea" was forthcoming, he grumbled at her and went to lie on the hearth rug.

Erin started preparing a late breakfast, hearing the shower shut off and, moments later, water running in the bathroom sink. She smiled a little. In her note she had invited him to use the shower and explained where a razor could be found; a pointed comment he had clearly taken to heart. He had also, judging by a missing cup and lowered level of coffee in the pot, taken his morning caffeine with him.

Erin had no dining table, but a breakfast bar formed a part of the partition and in between cooking chores she set out plates and silverware. By the time Matt Gavin came out of the bathroom, the main room of the cabin smelled enticingly of bacon and eggs and fresh homemade rolls.

Erin greeted him by saying "Hello" and taking away his coffee cup to refill. One quick glance had showed her that he was, clean and shaved, more than handsome. He was devastating.

It bothered her. Having lived with one extraordinary man and been exposed to many others, Erin had learned to mistrust extremes. It did no good to remind herself that this man's extraordinary looks could hardly be compared to Stuart's incredible, driven talent; it was, she knew, like comparing apples and oranges.

Still, she was only too aware that Matt Gavin lived in a fast-moving and high-powered world, and a wound she had believed healed cringed away from the threat of that world.

The calming peace she had found in the wilderness wrapped around her, protecting her from her body's tentative awareness of the presence of a devastating man.

So the clear, steady gray eyes that looked at her out of that handsome face found no interested awareness in her own gaze. She merely placed food before him, joined him at the bar, and began eating her breakfast.

After a moment he followed suit. After another moment he sent her a sideways glance. "You're a good cook," he noted.

"Thanks." Erin didn't look at him even though she was aware of his oblique glances.

He tried again. "Thanks for the use of your couch. And for washing the clothes, and the shower and breakfast."

"You're welcome."

He laughed suddenly, a short sound that was barely amused. "Hardly. Hardly welcome."

"You weren't invited," she reminded him.

Nothing more was said until the meal was finished. Erin poured more coffee for them, but took hers to the sink as she began cleaning up. Silent, he rose and began helping. She accepted the help matter-of-factly, but didn't comment on it. When they were finished, she took her cup into the living room, and he followed suit. She sat on one end of the couch; he took the other.

Erin began feeling amused, but didn't let it show. He was, she realized, trying to get some handle on her. Watching her every movement, bothered by her silence. And Erin, who was herself a student of people in spite of her lonely surroundings, half-consciously tried to fit him into a mental niche.

She was, she decided, not seeing him at his best. His best would be in an office or at a glittering cocktail party. His best would be three-piece suits and gleaming cars of foreign origin. His best would be room service and dim restaurants and laundry that was sent out unthinkingly and not hung on a line behind a cabin.

His best was certainly not dusty trips up mountains aboard bad-tempered roan horses, or shotguns fired without warning, or couches to sleep on, or uncommunicative women with whom to have breakfast.

Particularly the latter. Women who had breakfast with this man, she thought ruefully, probably scattered rose petals in his path — metaphorically speaking, of course. According to what Erin had read — and knew from experience — extraordinarily handsome men weren't always good lovers, but there was something about this one, something she sensed or just something in his eyes, that told her he understood women too well to be inept or selfish.

And if that wasn't a ridiculous thought, she mused uneasily, to be having about a stranger —

"What are you thinking?" he asked suddenly.

"I don't know you well enough to answer that," she said, her voice easy with an effort she hoped didn't show. "Thoughts aren't meant for strangers."

"You looked annoyed."

"Did I?"

He frowned a little. "You have," he said finally, consideringly, "gone to some lengths to make this entire morning painfully impersonal."

"I haven't gone to any lengths at all." She looked at him, smiled a twisted smile. "I am what I am, Mr. Gavin."

"Matt, for godsake. Calling me by my first name won't strike you mute."

Erin said nothing.

His frown deepened. "Look, will it kill you to talk to me like a reasonably friendly human being instead of regarding me as something your dog dragged in?"

"Have I done that? Sorry."

"You're so cool." He stared at her, a fixed gaze that probed and searched. "So — unflappable. Even yesterday, when you were tired." His eyes lifted to her bright hair confined high on her head and swinging free behind her, and there was speculation in his eyes.

As if, she thought, he were wondering at the common belief about red hair being a brand of passion. Now that was *another* peculiar thought, she realized uneasily.

And Erin was surprised to find herself briefly tempted to explain the coolness he commented on, the control. She frowned a bit, not pleased by the impulse, and said, "You should get started back to town. Don't worry about my horse; he's much calmer and easier to ride than the roan was. When you get to town, just tie the reins loosely to the saddlehorn and let him go. He'll come home."

Matt Gavin slowly finished his coffee,

never taking his eyes off her, then reached over to set the cup on the coffee table. Leaning back, he said musingly, "I heard about that reporter you chased off the mountain with a load of buckshot in his pants. Would you do that to me? I wonder. Just chase me off as if I were an annoyance to be dealt with?"

"Do you think I wouldn't?" she said.

"Oh, I think you would. I think it wouldn't matter to you a bit that I work for the company you write for." He paused, then went on deliberately. "What I'm wondering, really, is why. Why you're hiding up here. Why a beautiful, intelligent, talented woman would be so cold."

Erin knew he was trying to provoke her, probing for some reaction from her. She was, again briefly, tempted to tell him just why. Tempted to explain. But she was a private woman, and she said nothing.

"How old are you?" he asked abruptly.

"Twenty-eight." No hesitation, no evasion.

His eyes searched her impassive face. "When you signed the first contract four years ago," he said, "it was in another name. About three years ago, you explained in a letter that your name was now legally Scott." He hesitated for a moment. "You were married, weren't you?"

"I was married." She wondered absently why she was answering his questions, why she was just sitting here watching his face and feeling peculiarly detached.

"You're divorced now."

"Yes."

"How long were you married?"

"I lived with my husband for a year." Erin felt something gathering, tensing, threatening to spring from the dark closet where it lived. Matt Gavin, she realized dimly, was very good at probing. And all her instincts were shouting at her. She wanted to get up, walk away, to go and saddle a horse and put him on it and get him out of her life.

Because when dark things leaped from closets and stood nakedly between two strangers, they couldn't be strangers anymore.

"Just a year? You don't strike me as the kind to give up that easily."

She watched his eyes drop to her mouth, and realized that she was worrying her lower lip. Instantly, she stopped. Words came from somewhere and piled up in front of the closet to keep the dark thing trapped.

"Sometimes," she said, "it isn't a matter of giving up. Sometimes it's . . . recognition that there's nothing to fight for. Nothing

43

that matters anymore. Sometimes you just can't keep getting up when you're knocked down."

He frowned. "Do you mean —"

"I don't mean anything." She stood abruptly and carried their coffee cups to the kitchen.

"Erin . . ."

She started when the voice came from behind her, when he said her name. She felt curiously cold, but there was heat spreading over the surface of her body, skin tingling. Her knees were weak again, and her heart thudded against her ribs. Accustomed to digging for motivation in characters, accustomed to studying reactions objectively, she found her own reaction to him deeply disturbing.

What was wrong with her?

"Erin, I don't want to pry, but —"

"Then don't." She turned, suppressing an instinctive physical withdrawal when she saw how close to her he stood. Too close — he was too close to her. Too close to her pain. "Don't pry. Stop asking questions. You turn up on my porch one day and expect the story of my life the next?"

He nodded slowly. "All right, I had that coming. It's really none of my business, is it?"

"It's none of your business," she agreed.

He looked at her intently, searching her calm face and shuttered eyes. Wondering if a failed marriage had made her this way or if something else had been the cause.

Matt Gavin was a man who was comfortable with women, a man who understood women better than most. But this woman baffled him. There was something in her lovely, wary green eyes, a shadow of some dreadful hurt, and it touched something inside him.

He hadn't known her eyes would be green, or her hair red; only the features of her face were familiar to him — as familiar as his own. Her vivid coloring brought those features to life and indicated a passion otherwise deeply hidden . . . or unawakened. Her beauty and wariness had first drawn him, but it was that hidden passion which intrigued him.

Behind his immobile face, Matt's mind worked quickly. Everything inside him warned that his only chance was to make an impression on this guarded woman, and to make it quickly. She was adept at ridding herself of strangers.

He couldn't afford to remain one.

"I'm not normally so inquisitive," he murmured. "My only excuse is that I've never cared for shadow-boxing."

Erin thought she knew what he meant, but asked anyway. "Meaning?"

He crossed his arms over his broad chest and seemed to study her intently. "Well, when a man finds himself interested in a woman, he generally has to contend with her past, because he isn't a part of it. Unless she's a childhood sweetheart, in which case he *is* her past."

"You don't waste time with small talk, do you." It was an observation rather than a question.

"I can't afford to, can I? At any moment I may find myself tumbling down this mountain, speeded along by your shotgun."

"There is that." Erin found herself amused by his solemnity, but fought off the urge to relax and enjoy his approach. "Look, Mr. Gavin —"

"If," he interrupted conversationally, "you don't start calling me Matt, I'm going to kiss you silly."

She blinked. "Look, Matt —"

"Works every time," he told an invisible third party. "All you have to do is threaten them with a fate worse than death."

Erin bit the inside of her cheek and cleared her throat, staving off laughter. "Matt, I really hate to see a busy man waste time in a — lost cause. And I'd hate to endanger your future progeny by asking you to ride up the mountain every day, which you'd have to do since I rarely go down to town. So —"

"I thought I'd stay here."

It was, she realized, a very matter-of-fact statement. And his tone was so reasonable that Erin found herself unable to object. For a split second. "No."

"You have a very comfortable couch," he offered hopefully. "And since I've already spent one night here, your virtuous reputation in town is likely shot to hell anyway."

"You slept on my couch, and Jake knows it; he'll spread the word." She was amused to find herself patiently explaining things to him. "But you can't stay here."

"Jake." Momentarily distracted, he assumed an expression of irritation. "He's the one who rented me *that horse?*"

By the tone of voice, Erin gathered Matt had not been overly fond of the roan; he must have spent an uncomfortable couple of days aboard the animal. "He's the one," she told him.

"I have a score to settle with that young man."

Erin smiled a little. "Be careful how you settle it. Jake's older than he looks, and he was a marine." She considered a moment, then added thoughtfully, "And he seems guileless; don't drink his moonshine if he offers it."

"Too late." Matt's expression spoke plainly of remembered agony. "I sampled the stuff before I got on that horse. Why hasn't Jake been arrested for peddling poison?"

"We like him," Erin replied simply. "Besides, we know better than to drink it."

"So he springs it on unsuspecting strangers," Matt realized with a sigh.

"Something like that."

He brooded on the thought for a few moments, then dismissed it. "Anyway, if Jake's your pipeline into town, he can report that I'm still sleeping on the couch."

"What's believed for one night," she said very dryly, "won't be believed for several." And was ignored.

"I've always wanted to spend time in — the back of beyond." He looked around the cozy cabin. "The wilderness stops at your door from the looks of it; you've got all the creature comforts."

"No," she said.

"I would, of course," he said, "pitch in for groceries and whatever. Board."

"No."

48

"We can talk about your next book."

"No, Matt," she said firmly.

He looked at her for a moment unreadably. "Well, at least you used my name," he said. "Unprompted, as it were. That's something."

Perversely, she found herself wishing she had not been quite so uncompromising. Still . . . "Sorry, Matt. I just don't want a guest." Strongly suspecting she'd end in defeat if she allowed the "conversation" to go on any longer, she moved around him toward the back door. "I'll saddle the horse for you."

"Do I have to leave now?"

Erin hardened her heart, which was difficult in the face of his questionable meekness. "Yes. I have things to do; I've been away for two weeks, and I have work to catch up on."

He followed her out to the barn. "Well, thanks for the hospitality, Erin."

She was busy brushing Amos, but spared a moment to direct a suspicious look at Matt's guileless expression. "Uh-huh." She had the vague feeling that the man was hugely enjoying some private joke — at her expense.

There was just something about his meekness, she thought uneasily. Like the earlier sheepishness, it had a motive under it. She couldn't think what it could be, but her knees felt weak again. Dammit. Those gray eyes . . .

A few moments later she led the saddled horse from the barn and watched while Matt climbed aboard — with grace if not with expertise. He held the reins in one hand, gazing down at her for a moment.

"Just tie the reins and turn him loose once I reach town?" he questioned, and when she nodded, nodded himself. "Fine. Thanks again, Erin. Bye."

She watched him ride away, thinking nothing, ignoring a peculiar feeling of depression. When he disappeared from her sight and the peaceful mountain sounds were all to be heard, she shook her head and went into the cabin.

Odd that it felt so empty.

Erin kept herself busy for the remainder of the day. She worked outside for the most part, replenishing bird feeders, repairing the fence around her small kitchen garden, and working in the garden itself.

Amos came home late in the afternoon, moving briskly and obviously glad to return. She unsaddled him, reflecting with a pang that it really was too much to expect that any man would spend the better part of a day on a horse just to visit a woman. Only ten miles or so to town, true, but given the terrain, a trip up and down on horseback took most of a day.

Grimacing at her own dim disappointment, Erin fed and watered her horses, then went into the cabin to feed Chester and herself. She worked for a while that night in the peaceful quiet of her study, getting her notes and research organized for the next book.

Like everything else in the cabin that was not made by herself, her computer had been transported up the mountain at considerable expense, and she used it carefully. Her generator was a powerful one, but during this time of year unpredictable and sometimes violent storms could easily cut her off from everyone and everything for weeks at a time; unwilling to be without power for lack of fuel, Erin tended to be miserly in her use of any appliance that consumed electricity — particularly the computer.

She did all of her planning, therefore, on paper, organizing as much as possible so that her actual writing utilized "quality" time. Somewhat to her surprise, Erin had found that her work went much more smoothly in this way; she wasted little time while actually writing on the computer, since her books were roughed out in some detail in longhand on paper.

She worked in preparation that night, her bright desk lamp throwing crouching shadows around the room. Neither the quiet nor the shadows disturbed Erin; she worked steadily, only half-hearing Chester's soft snores from where he lay by the door. She rose a few times to consult books on the crowded shelves lining three walls of the study, arranged her notes, and constructed a brief outline to be filled in during the next few days.

She hoped.

It was late when she tidied her desk and quit for the night. She went through her usual getting-ready-for-bed routine, and it was only when she was in bed and drowsy that thoughts of Matt Gavin crept into her mind.

At one moment half asleep, she found herself abruptly wide awake and restless the next. From experience, she knew it would be almost impossible to blank her mind; a mind accustomed to the ongoing creative process, she'd discovered, was often obsessive. She had spent many a sleepless night listening to her mind work through a story.

This was, however, the first time in a long time that something other than a story had kept her awake and thinking.

She lay there, staring up at a dark ceiling, and swore at herself solemnly. Facing her thoughts with reluctant honesty, she admitted that Matt had made a strong impression on her. Not his looks especially, she decided, because she had known many handsome and charismatic men — particularly during her whirlwind courtship and marriage.

No, she thought, it was something else, something besides his looks. He had a certain presence; in spite of the fact that her own sharpened instincts had marked him as a man out of his element, there was something about him that seemed curiously adaptable.

Unwilling to draw comparisons, she nonetheless found herself doing just that. Stuart had not been adaptable; remove him from his element, and he was clearly a fish out of water. He had been comfortable, even brilliant, in his own world, and totally at a loss out of it. Coping masterfully and enjoyably with his frenetic lifestyle, he had been bored and moody in rare moments of quiet, and explosively temperamental when his will was thwarted.

Matt Gavin, Erin thought reluctantly, would not be that kind of man. And where

Stuart was an essentially humorless man, she thought that Matt had not only a sense of humor but also a strong sense of the ridiculous and an ability to laugh at himself.

More than a little surprised that her opinion of Matt should have developed so strongly and after so short a time, Erin frowned in the darkness. Fiercely pushing him from her mind, she closed her eyes and counted sheep.

And it wasn't ten minutes later that she found herself half-giggling and feeling the heat of self-consciousness in her face as she realized that her stubborn thoughts had taken a gentle turn into the speculative: She wondered what Matt Gavin would be like as a lover.

She had never considered herself a passionate woman sexually; Stuart's love-making had been as frantic and as overpowering as the man himself, leaving her breathless but, on some deep level, unfulfilled. At times rough, always unpredictable, he had been a slightly selfish lover, concerned first with his own pleasure. She had often longed just to be held in loving silence, but had more often than not found herself gazing at his back as they lay in their bed. Or worse, gazing at the ceiling as she lay there alone, because Stuart had barely caught his breath before leaving her to pursue a fleeting idea.

Alone now, she stared at the ceiling and wondered about Matt Gavin, unable to halt the speculation. Would he, she wondered, leave a lover in her lonely bed with nothing more than an absent kiss? Would his passion explode with no warning, overpowering but not satisfying? Did a demon drive him to be rough and frantic in love as in life? Or would he be a sensitive and generous lover, evoking tenderness as well as desire?

The thoughts that had flickered that morning rose again now with certainty. No, she thought, Matt would not be a selfish lover, or rough or impatient. She was uncomfortable with that knowledge, that certainty, but didn't doubt it. Somehow, she just knew.

He was an undeniably, heart-stoppingly masculine man who, either by instinct or experience, understood and appreciated women. It was in his eyes.

"It's in your imagination," she told herself fiercely aloud, startled by the sound of her own voice.

Erin turned, pounding her pillow and swearing unsteadily. Too late, she thought, for regrets. Too late to wish she had encouraged his interest. He would have been safe, she thought dimly, as a lover, because he had his own life in New York and would have returned there, leaving her with what might have been a good memory and her peace intact.

There would have been no threat to her heart or her life, just an interlude like a stirring breeze soon gone.

No threat . . .

Erin found depression hanging over her head like a gloomy cloud the next morning. She did her usual chores automatically and with no enthusiasm, disquieted at her unusual brooding. She gave the cabin a thorough cleaning, working hard and quickly to block thoughts. By ten a.m. the cabin was spotless, and she was still depressed.

The radio squawked as she was passing listlessly to take her coffee out onto the porch, and she detoured to answer the unusual summons, half-expecting Mal to announce a package or something awaiting her in town.

He didn't.

"Erin . . . this dude who went up to see you —"

She felt interest quicken. "What about him, Mal?"

"Well, did you tell him not to come back?

56

I mean, are you expecting him up there again?"

Erin frowned at her friend's faintly unsteady tone. "I'm not expecting him, but I didn't threaten him with the shotgun if he came back. Why?"

"He's — uh — a resourceful man, your dude. The whole town's tickled about it."

"About what?"

Mal didn't have to answer, because that was when she heard the music.

Chapter Three

It began first as more of a throbbing than a sound, a vibration felt rather than heard. Erin signed off the radio with a hasty, abrupt good-bye and carried her coffee out to the front porch, baffled. She stood there for a moment before the throbbing became sounds, and identification of those sounds did nothing to stop her bewilderment.

Ravel's *Bolero*?

It was, confusingly, just that, and the music swelled steadily, blotting out all the gentle sounds of nature. There was another sound accompanying the music, a sound Erin couldn't identify at first; when she could identify it, bewilderment clashed with incredulity.

A helicopter?

So it proved to be, and a helicopter, moreover, with character. It was painted a vile green that shocked the eyes and would cause any self-respecting soul to cringe. It was obviously vintage army surplus, a great hulking gunship bare of guns and boasting definitely obscene graffiti painted in various colors. It thundered over the cabin, blaring Ravel from a loudspeaker bolted near its blunt nose, and set down with a thump drowned by music about twenty yards from the cabin — as far away as it could get without tangling with trees or falling off the mountain.

Erin held on to one of the posts supporting the overhang on her porch, dimly aware that her mouth was open and instinctively bracing herself against the rush of oily wind caused by the thumping rotors.

While she watched in astonishment, Matt Gavin climbed from the aircraft and strolled toward her with complete sang-froid as the peculiar green machine at his back lifted again with a roar and swooped off still blaring the seductive *Bolero*.

On the corner of the porch Chester snored contentedly, never stirring at the noise or the cessation of it.

"Hi," Matt said casually as he reached the porch.

On some faraway level of herself, Erin realized then why the entire town had been, in Mal's words, tickled. She could easily imagine the faces of townspeople when that nauseating helicopter had set down near the small motel where Matt had undoubtedly stayed. Especially if it had announced its arrival there with the same sort of fanfare.

She stared at him, stunned and incredulous, feeling sudden laughter welling up. "You — you —" She didn't even know what she *wanted* to say.

Matt was no help at all. Deadpan, he gazed at her, arms crossed over his chest. He looked neither defiant nor amused, simply calm.

Erin sat down on the porch, put her coffee to one side, and laughed herself silly. When she finally got herself under control, she wiped streaming eyes and found Matt sitting beside her, grinning.

"Oh, Lord," she gasped. "Who picked the music?"

Laughter gleamed in his eyes. "Me. Didn't have much choice, I'm afraid. It was either Ravel or some godawful marching music. As you can see — and hear — Steve likes to announce his arrival."

Erin held her aching stomach, smiling at him unconsciously. "The pilot? Where on earth did you find him?"

"He's an old friend of mine. Lives in Denver. He owns a successful charter service. I called him this morning and asked if he'd mind being my taxi for a while, since I'd met a fascinating woman who lived in an aerie, and I didn't want to end up impaired for life and permanently bowlegged."

Erin choked.

"He said," Matt went on blandly, "he would happily deliver me every morning you cared to have me, then retrieve me before dark. I'm paying for fuel, and Steve is gleeful at the opportunity to shock people with that monstrosity he fondly calls Sadie."

A little weakly, Erin said, "It'll cost you a fortune — even if it's deductible as transportation costs to find a reclusive writer."

Matt smiled at her slowly. "Oh, Salem isn't paying. I also called them this morning and announced that I was on vacation."

Erin shut her mouth and tried to think. "But you — I mean — you can't want to —"

"What I'd like to do," he interrupted smoothly, "is find out why one of my favorite writers requested several postponements on her last deadline, and seems to be . . . unable to tell us anything about her work-in-progress. That's not like you, Erin."

She had to mentally shift gears from the personal to the professional, and felt a bit chagrined about it. Though apparently footing the bill for his transport, Matt Gavin was obviously here for purely business reasons. She was irritated with herself for being upset by that.

Matt watched the play of emotions on her lovely face, his heart leaping as he realized that he had already made an impression on Erin. But he pushed eagerness aside, all too aware that there was still a way to go yet. "Writer's block?" he asked neutrally.

Instantly, she said, "That's a catch-all phrase, and you know it. Writers get *blocked* on particular stories, maybe, and occasionally burn out on the work altogether." She picked up her coffee cup and frowned at it, trying to keep her mind on professional matters and ignore those other more nebulous thoughts. "And maybe I haven't talked about what I'm working on because it hasn't taken shape yet."

"Have you worked lately?"

"Last night."

"And?"

"And what?" Erin felt defensive and tried to ignore the vague uneasiness that had plagued her for the past three months. Tried to ignore her bitter certainty that the notes and summary she'd compiled roughed-out a story that was pure garbage.

"How did it go?" Matt was gazing straight ahead, apparently at nothing, his expression neutral.

"I don't want to talk about it," she said, abrupt.

He was silent for a long moment, still gazing ahead. Then he said, "All right, we'll talk about something else. I need your help, Erin. Tell me how to box shadows. Tell me how to fight my way through some other man's stupid mistakes."

She turned her head to stare at him. He wasn't — surely he wasn't — he didn't mean — She cut off the confused thoughts. It didn't make sense. *He* didn't make sense. "I don't know," she said carefully, "what you mean."

"I have a thing about redheads."

Erin blinked. Good heavens, she thought, he did mean — "I thought this was a professional visit," she managed in a very steady voice.

"I'm on vacation, remember?" Matt was smiling just a little, but still not looking at her.

"You asked about my work."

"Yes. And we'll talk about that again. When you're ready."

He was, she thought, simply interested in the work. The work that had provided quite a bit of income for his company during the past few years. There was a bitter taste in her mouth, and she wondered tiredly if she was destined to be exploited by the men in her life. Instantly, she qualified that thought.

Matt was not "the man" in her life, and Stuart had not exploited her. Not that. Not quite that.

Erin took a deep breath. "I see."

"No, I don't think you do." He looked at her then, with quiet, level gray eyes. "Your work is important to me, Erin, but only because it's a part of you. Because you're a *writer*. Not because you make money for my company."

She stared at him, suddenly puzzled by some inflection in his voice. "Your company."

He hesitated, then grinned faintly. "My company. I don't suppose any of us ever notices who signs our checks."

Erin remembered then. "My God — you own Salem."

Matt nodded.

"And you expect me to believe you don't care about the earnings from my books?"

"It does sound unlikely, doesn't it?" He seemed to think about that, to find it amusing. "But true, whether you believe it or not. Erin, I'll release you from your contract if you like. You can sign with another publisher."

"And?" She looked at him warily.

"And I'll still be on vacation. Still around. And I still want to talk to you about your

64

work when you're ready."

"Why? Why would it interest you if I were writing for someone else?"

He was silent for a moment, reaching into his pocket for cigarettes and lighter. "You don't smoke, do you?" he asked idly, and when she shook her head, added, "It's a lousy habit."

Erin waited patiently.

Matt lighted the cigarette and smoked for a moment in silence, then sighed. "You," he said, "are a writer. It comes across in every word you write. It isn't a job with you; it isn't a profession. It's what you are. You put your heart and soul into a book, and it shows."

She felt more than a little shaken. How could he know? Was it so obvious that every word mattered to her? "Assuming —" She cleared her throat. "Assuming that's true, my question stands. Why would you be interested if — if —"

"If I didn't stand to gain?" His smile was crooked. "Erin, I have all the money I'll ever need. Believe it or not, what matters to me are the writers."

Erin looked at him curiously. Sales didn't matter? Money didn't matter? It was, she thought, an unorthodox attitude — to say the least. Unless . . . "Have you — ever written?" she asked.

"Why do you ask?"

"You *have* written." The evasion, obscurely, pleased her.

He shrugged. "Years ago. I found out I wasn't a born writer. Oh, I could write to please readers. But my basic pleasure in writing was a fascination with the whole process. From the origin of an idea to the finished product on the shelves."

Erin dredged into her memories of what she'd read and heard about Salem. "You took over Salem about ten years ago, didn't you? And the first crop of books you bought hit the best-seller lists — a first for the company."

Matt dropped his cigarette into the dirt in front of the steps and reached a booted toe to ground it out. "I publish what I like."

"First-time authors, most of them," she noted. It was coming back to her now, what she'd read about her publisher. That he was tough in a tough business, but fiercely supportive of his writers — of all writers. Salem paid writers well, and treated them with an unusual amount of respect in a business where books and authors had come to be packaged and promoted like soap powder and breakfast cereal.

It was, basically, why she had submitted

her first book to Salem; she had checked the market critically and had heard again and again that Salem was a home for its writers rather than a place where one sent manuscripts and from which one received checks.

"Writers have it rough in today's market," Matt mused almost to himself. "So many houses want their — products — tailored to whatever happens to be popular at the moment. Good writing is sacrificed in favor of homogenized banality. House policy dictates that editors tone down this, cut that, reword this phrase because it isn't *acceptable* as it stands —

"We have books available for every taste," Matt said, his level voice roughening, anger creeping into the tone. "And writers are being squeezed into molds. You don't buy many books on their own merits anymore; you buy a *kind* of book. Look at the top six best sellers any given month, and at least four of them look mass-produced! Dammit, books can be entertaining without being trash.

"Writers should be left alone to explore their potential, should be encouraged to write what they feel — and they should be paid for the effort! Numbers should never be the judge of accomplishment, and houses should never restrict a writer's vision just because it doesn't match their own —"

Matt broke off abruptly and laughed. He looked at Erin, no apology or defiance in his expression, but rather a faintly amused self-mockery. "Sorry. Didn't mean to get on my soapbox."

Erin drew a deep breath. "Lord, don't apologize," she said, sounding as dazed as she felt. "What you believe would be music to any writer's ears. I had no idea . . . Talk like that at any writer's conference, and they'd be beating down your door."

He smiled. "Luckily, I have the capital to gamble. If Salem loses money, I can poke more into the company. But we haven't lost money yet — which proves, I believe, that writers and books don't have to fit into molds to find an audience."

Erin shook her head, bemused. Offhand, she couldn't recall ever meeting anyone — particularly a businessman — who seemed more concerned with talent than with the product of that talent. "You're . . . an unusual man," she said slowly.

Matt shrugged. "Not really. Even businessmen can be idealistic; it's just that most of them have to think about earning a living and listening to a boss."

She looked at him, realizing that she still was not certain just what interested Matt

Gavin here in Colorado: her or her writing. And she was startled when he seemingly picked up on her confusion, almost as if he could read her mind.

"I want to spend time with you, Erin. Is that so hard to understand?"

"Why — professionally?"

He nodded slightly, his expression clearly saying that she was right to divide his motives into professional and personal. "Professionally . . . because you're a born writer apparently having trouble writing — for whatever reason. And I've had some success in helping writers over walls; I want to help you if I can. Personally . . ."

"Because you have a thing about redheads?" she ventured when his voice trailed off.

He hesitated, gazing out over the loneliness of the place she had chosen to call home. "I could say it was because you had to fasten those buttons," he murmured.

"Would that be true?" she asked steadily. She remembered her gaping pajama top and his fascinated gaze, her heart leaping at the realization that he had found her attractive — even if it was only physically.

"Partly. But even before that . . . even seeing you wearing jeans and a flannel shirt, I was drawn to you. You made me think of a rose bush in full bloom. Very lovely — and potentially painful. Some roses have more thorns than others; you'd better wear gloves when you touch them. That's you."

Erin was a little surprised by the analogy, and unsure whether to be flattered or insulted. "So you put on gloves?" she asked, carefully polite.

"Well, I think I'd better. At least until I find out if you're prickly because you're a writer, or because of something else. Given my druthers, I wouldn't get involved with a writer." He sent her a swift smile. "Temperamental creatures, writers. But I don't seem to have a choice where you're concerned. If you want me out of your life, Erin, you'll have to use that shotgun. I won't go willingly."

Erin returned the steady gaze, her thoughts and emotions chasing themselves in circles. Her gaze wavered and focused on something in the distance as she remembered her thoughts and regrets of the night before. She was, it seemed, being given a chance for that interlude she'd wondered about.

He was safe, she thought. Safe. He'd get bored in time, and go home to his city life. It was bound to happen. And three years of private peace had strengthened her; she could cope, now, with a relationship — a fleeting one. Couldn't she?

She wondered, then, if the failure of her marriage had marked her indelibly; would she always, forever, question her own ability to cope? Could she never be sure of herself? Had Stuart drained away even confidence in herself?

"How he must have hurt you," Matt said quietly.

She started in surprise.

"Shadows," he said. "In your eyes. I wonder if I'm any good at shadowboxing."

"Matt, I don't . . ."

"I've already put on the gloves, Erin. The boxing gloves — and the gloves to handle thorns. Are you going for the gun? Or should I square off and start fighting?"

"Damn you," she said.

Correctly interpreting that muttered curse, he smiled again, eyes steady. "I don't suppose you'd like to shine a light on those shadows and make it easier for me?"

"If you shine a light on shadows, they disappear," she managed carefully.

"I know."

He was safe, she told herself fiercely. Safe.

Erin held her voice even. "Matt, I won't — I won't chase you off with a shotgun. But I — don't know you."

He was silent for a moment, obviously thinking that over. When he spoke, it was in a quiet tone. "But you'll give us a chance to get to know each other?"

She nodded, not hesitant, but silent. Wondering if the kindest lesson Stuart had taught her had been to never again throw her entire heart into a relationship. She wouldn't, she decided, do that again. Not this time. This time she would still be whole when it was over.

He rose and drew her to her feet so that they both stood at the bottom step. "That's all I'm asking, Erin. A chance. If I ask questions you don't want to answer, then don't. If I say or do something you don't like, tell me. As long as you'll give us a chance."

Erin could hardly help but think how different this beginning was from the last one. She felt absurdly grateful to Matt for the patience he promised. And he must have seen that.

"I'm breaking new ground?" he asked gently.

Even that mild question almost caused her to withdraw, but then, with a feeling of release, she knew she would answer. "Something like that." She nodded jerkily and stepped away from him, retrieving her hands from his quiet grasp and sliding them into the pockets of her jeans.

"He swept you off your feet?"

That question, like the first, was mild and undemanding, and his expression was neutral but intent. The lack of demand and the lack of persuasion allowed her to answer with no feeling of being forced against her will.

"Like a steamroller." Erin found herself smiling ruefully. "They say every girl hopes Prince Charming will come along on his charger and carry her away; I can tell you it isn't all it's cracked up to be. Princes can be imperious . . . and falling off a charger hurts like hell."

"Did he rescue you from a dragon?" Matt was smiling.

She laughed a little. "No. No dragon. I wasn't running away from anything; I had loving parents and a good home. I didn't think there was anything missing until he came riding by all white and shining, and made the rest of the world look dark and slow and dull."

"And then? Did the prince get tarnished?"

Almost absently, Erin began walking, and he fell into step beside her. She followed a favorite path that wound gradually farther up the mountain, thinking that the light and casual talk of princes made it easier to talk of difficult things. Did Matt realize that? Probably. Certainly.

"No," she said at last, dryly. "He didn't get tarnished. He didn't change at all. He had feet of clay, like all princes; I just couldn't see that at first. The shine of him blinded me. He threw me across his saddle and galloped off, and I was so breathless and grateful."

"Why grateful?" Matt was still neutral, still calm.

"Every girl wants a prince." She shrugged, mocking herself faintly. "And I got one. A handsome, talented prince who could — and did — set the world on fire with his brilliance."

After a moment Matt said, "May I ask — ?"

"Stuart Travis." There was another long moment of silence. Erin didn't look at Matt, but she could feel his surprised recognition of that name.

"Quite a brilliant prince." His voice was still calm, reflective. "Singer, songwriter, world-famous entertainer. If I remember correctly, he's won more awards than any other singer in history."

"He has. He's thirty-six." She related the information calmly, with no envy or bitterness in her tone. "He's been a genius all his life, and his star keeps on climbing. Years ago a reporter realized in shock that Stuart had written, recorded, and performed eight out of ten of the top songs for the past decade. A remarkable achievement."

"A . . . driven genius."

Erin glanced at him, curiously not surprised by his perception. "Driven by powerful demons. Temperamental, moody, constantly creative. Burning continually like a comet, rushing through space and time as if there weren't enough of either." Softly, she added, "I could never catch my breath."

After a moment of silence, Matt returned them impassively to the safety of analogy. "So the prince just kept charging through life. And what about the princess?"

Erin laughed under her breath, wryly amused at herself as she hadn't been then. "She didn't get to live in her castle. She got a succession of hotel rooms and learned to live out of a suitcase. She ate her meals courtesy of room service or takeout places because the prince was too famous and too restless to eat in restaurants and too impatient to let her cook."

She stopped walking, looking out over the spectacular view where the path ended; they were miles in the air, looking down at a distant world. Vaguely, she wondered if that accounted for her fondness for this place; it was above the world. Unreachable.

"Hard to share a genius with the world," Matt commented, a faint question in his voice.

Erin shook her head, gazing blindly out on all that distance. "There was never anything to share. Never a part of him that was mine, I was . . . just there." She looked at Matt suddenly, and her smile twisted. "He loved me."

Matt frowned slightly. "But — ?"

Flatly, she explained what had taken her many long and painful months to realize and understand. "But he used me, used what he felt for me. Like everything else in his life. Fodder for his songs. He tore emotions to shreds — his and others' — to find songs. He demanded. And what he got, he chewed up and spit out to the world in a song. And he never gave in any other way. The world could have what he was, what he felt, but those closest to him could only give and give until he couldn't drain them anymore."

Matt reached out suddenly and pulled her into his arms, holding her with a fierce gentleness. "I'm sorry, Erin," he said huskily.

She put her arms around his lean waist,

holding him because she needed that contact, hiding her face against his neck. "Not a cruel prince," she said unsteadily. "Not deliberately cruel. Just driven. He was what he had to be, what his talent made him be. Still is, I guess. And I couldn't give anymore. I didn't have anything left. I —" She broke off abruptly, unwilling to explain what had finally broken her, what had collapsed the empty shell she had become.

Matt stroked her long hair gently and held her with no demand and no more questions. "No wonder you came up here," he said finally, quiet. "And no wonder you're so wary. You've already given more than anyone should ever have asked of you."

She stood in the quiet embrace for long moments, feeling peculiarly suspended and not a little shocked. A stranger. He was a *stranger,* and she'd told him things even her parents had not been told. She pulled away slightly and gazed up at that handsome, still face, unable to guess what he was thinking, unable to see what lay behind the quiet of his gray eyes.

"I don't —" she began in a troubled voice, but Matt interrupted.

"You don't talk about it, do you? But you told me." He smiled down at her. "You needed to tell someone, Erin, that's all. It was time for you to tell someone. I happened to be here, and asked."

She was surprised again. Was she so transparent that he saw she needed reassurance? Or was he that perceptive? Still bothered by her willingness to tell him what she had told no one else, Erin was only partly aware that he had turned them back toward the cabin. She was very aware that as they walked he kept one arm loosely around her shoulders.

Safe . . . he was safe . . .

Abruptly, she said, "You don't know what I gave Stuart. What he — took. For all you know, I may well have been the proverbial misunderstood wife. A brilliant, talented husband, no room in his spotlight for me. For all you know, I could have run like a coward from my own imagination."

"You didn't."

"You can't *know* that," she insisted fiercely. They had reached the cabin, and she shrugged off his arm, turning to face him. "I don't want you to get the wrong idea, Matt. Don't think I'm some poor, wounded creature in need of sympathy and solace. Don't think I need another prince on another charger." She stopped, stared at him, realized what she'd said, and what it implied. "I don't believe in fairy tales anymore," she ended in a whisper.

Matt reached up to slide a hand beneath the heavy weight of her hair, a warm hand with no pressure. "I'm not offering fairy tales, Erin," he said quietly. "When I look at you, I don't see some frail maiden in need of a prince and cotton batting to be wrapped in. I see a woman to walk beside a man, not behind him. I see a wary woman who's been hurt, but not a weak woman."

He smiled at her slowly. "A woman who would never have run from a man or a marriage, except as a last resort. Stop doubting yourself, Erin."

"Have you ever been in love?" she asked him.

He hesitated, shook his head. "No. I have no scars from a past."

"The scars don't hurt. They're just reminders of mistakes. I wanted you to know. I won't make those mistakes again. I won't let myself be hurt like that again."

"You think I'd hurt you?"

"How can I know that?" She was honest. "I only know that I won't let you hurt me. Or anyone hurt me." She turned away from him again, looking toward the porch and Chester, and wondering dimly how her faithful canine friend could possibly be sleeping through so traumatic a moment.

Easily. It wasn't his trauma.

"Erin?"

She leaned down to pick up her discarded coffee cup, then half-turned back to look at him.

"Now you're running," he said.

She didn't deny the quiet accusation; she just gazed at him steadily. After a long moment she said, "When Stuart and I met, he wrote a song about us. I was flattered. I always thought that a man singing to a woman was corny — but when you're in love, nothing's corny. That song hit the top ten; millions of people heard it. Shortly after that we had our first fight — and millions of people heard it. Later. During a live concert. In a song."

Matt's brows drew together. "You mean he —"

"Fodder for his songs. The fighting . . . the making-up. Everything that we were was set to music and sung to the world. He — he wrote songs about our lovemaking. About sleepy eyes in the morning. About a peach nightgown I wore. About — being torn between his wife . . . and another woman."

She felt the hot sting of tears, but smiled faintly. "I didn't need to stand in his spotlight; he focused it on me. Stripped me naked in front of the world. I ran. Oh, I ran."

"I wouldn't do that to you, Erin," Matt said, something intense in his level tone.

"You don't have to run from me."

"Don't I? It would have been so much simpler, Matt, if . . . If you'd just seen those unfastened buttons. There's no threat in that. That's two people — finding something without having to look too deep. I thought you were safe. Here for a while and then . . . gone. No threat. But you want — something else. Don't you?"

"Yes," he said steadily.

She nodded a little. "Yes. Probing like that. Shadowboxing. To have something simple, you wouldn't have to fight." She paused, thinking, acknowledging her own vulnerability. "Funny that I know that." He had hardly touched her, yet she knew. She went into the cabin, carrying her coffee cup to the kitchen, knowing he was following.

She spoke before he could. "I think you're a wizard. I didn't want to — It was so damned *emotional* with Stuart. Euphoric highs and devastating lows — and no in between. I didn't want to feel like that again. I don't know if I can stand feeling like that again."

"So you just want something nonthreatening this time. Something simple. Something physical. And when it's over — an empty bed, but not an empty heart. Is that it?"

81

Erin couldn't tell from his voice how he was reacting to that. Without looking at him, she went into the living room, moving restlessly, aware that he was standing only feet away and watching her. "It sounds so — crude, put like that," she said in a low voice.

Matt felt the ache in his jaw, realizing only then that his teeth were gritted. Consciously, he relaxed his expression even as he leashed a very primitive desire to snatch whatever he could get. Not yet, he knew. Not just yet.

Fighting himself, determined that she wouldn't be rid of him so easily, his own emotions crept into his voice. "It is crude."

She swung around, staring at him now, surprised by the harshness of his voice. She felt abruptly defensive, uncertain. "Maybe — maybe I just want to take this time." She forced a short laugh. "Matt, I'm trying to be honest. If you want an affair, I won't — I can't — say no. I have both feet firmly on the ground this time, you see. Men and women . . . there's no magical mystery; people are attracted to one another. Either they do something about it, or they don't."

Erin squared her shoulders and held his impassive gaze. "I'd be sorry if you left, Matt, but I won't let you destroy my peace."

"Is it peace? Or a limbo?"

"Whatever it is," she said steadily, not rising to the bait, "I'm happy with it."

Matt crossed his arms over his broad chest and stared at her, no expression at all on his handsome face. "And you don't believe a polite, civilized, impersonal affair will disturb your peace? Is that it?"

Defiant now, feeling oddly in the wrong, Erin lifted her chin. "No. I don't."

"Okay."

She blinked. "What?"

"I said okay." He glanced around in a businesslike manner. "You have a radio, don't you? The grocer down in town mentioned something about it."

"I — yes, I do." Tensely, she gestured toward the small room containing the radio. "But why do you —"

"I'll get in touch with Steve and have him bring my stuff up from town." He paused to lift an eyebrow at her. "I can't stay away from New York indefinitely, so we may as well get on with it, right? No sense in keeping that motel room."

"I —"

"Of course, the whole town will know about us, but I don't suppose you care about that. I'll be gone in a couple of weeks anyway; they'll find something else to talk about then." Briskly, he headed for the radio.

Erin paced the living room, her emotions in turmoil. She heard his deep voice in the other room, and when he returned, she whirled to face him with an accusation.

"You said you wouldn't push!"

Matt looked at her in mild surprise. "But that was before I knew you wanted only an affair, Erin. Affairs tend to be quick things, you know; they start and they end — there isn't much in between. Surface, mostly. And since we both agree on the ground rules, what's the sense in waiting?"

Erin wanted very badly to have the courage of her convictions. He was offering what she had claimed to want, after all. She wanted to agree with him, to nod practically and say of course he was right, and why should they waste time?

She couldn't say it.

In a tone very different from the brisk one of before, Matt said, "It isn't what you want, is it?"

Chapter Four

"Damn you."

Matt smiled a little, for the first time since they had entered the cabin. "Maybe it wouldn't cut up your peace too much, Erin, but you don't want . . . just an affair."

She looked at him, suddenly curious, realizing how easily he could have taken her up on the offer. "And you don't want one either?"

"No."

"Then what do you want?" she asked in what was very nearly a wail. "You've put me through more emotions in an hour than I've had to cope with in three years! I don't understand! You say my books don't interest you commercially, even though my writing *does* interest you — so I assume you aren't up here offering a little R and R to the troops!"

Matt burst out laughing. Erin glared at him for a moment, then smiled reluctantly herself. She felt as if she'd been through a wringer since that helicopter had landed, and she hadn't the faintest idea how this man's mind worked.

It was, she realized, a reversal of the first day; he had been puzzled by her then, but the shoe was on the other foot now. He seemed to understand her, and she was bewildered by him.

"What I want," he said, smiling at her, "is to get to know a rather beautiful woman who's as prickly as a very thorny rose. I'll probably end up getting myself skewered, but I'm willing to take that chance. If, that is, I can convince her that I don't wade into relationships swinging a baseball bat or make it a practice to strip away the privacy of just anyone at all."

He crossed the room to stand before her, looking at her gravely. "Erin, I'd be as blind and deaf as a post if I didn't want to spend the rest of the day in your bed making love with you. And I'm neither blind nor deaf. But the *last* thing I want is to have you believe that another man is using you — for whatever reasons. When we make love, it'll be because we want to, for all the reasons that bring two people together. Not because a physical relationship is easier than an emotional one and less troublesome. Not because we want to avoid the clutter of emotions."

Erin felt her heart turn over as she gazed

up at him. "You," she said carefully, "are an anachronism. Or else," she added, "you've perfected the best and most original approach I've ever been privileged to hear."

"Don't lump me into the predatory-male group, please," he requested mildly. "I don't like labels. Besides, if you'd read the latest studies, you'd know that men tend to want emotional ties in a relationship. Nobody wants to sleep with a stranger if there's an alternative."

She looked at him for a moment, then caught her breath as he reached out and pulled her firmly into his arms. She couldn't seem to get her breath back, too conscious was she of the hard-muscled strength of his body pressed against hers. And her knees were weak again.

"Have you," he murmured, "ever heard the expression 'priming the pump'?"

Erin swallowed. "Uh-huh. It means to get something started."

"It's always nice to have one's actions understood," Matt said meditatively, and bent his head to hers.

Erin didn't know what she had expected to feel; other than her speculative thoughts of the day before, she'd not actually considered what it might be like to be kissed by Matt Gavin. But she had not, certainly, expected to feel something entirely new to her. She had not expected to discover with a shock that she was indeed a passionate woman — with this man, at least.

Shaken, she was only dimly aware that her arms had risen to encircle his neck, only faintly and bemusedly aware of feeling small in his embrace. Confused, she wondered how she could feel so small when she knew she *wasn't* . . . and what was this man doing to her?

Matt didn't waste time with gentleness, although there was nothing rough or crude in his kiss. He kissed her with a force and passion that demanded, yet did not take. He parted her lips with fierce need, yet it was not the plundering kiss of a victor; it was not possession but persuasion, fervent and urgent.

Erin, suddenly dizzy, felt the force of that kiss. She felt the persuasion that was insidiously heating her blood and draining the strength — what little was left — from her legs.

And though she was astonished at the realization, Erin knew that she was being, for the second time in her life, swept off her feet. But this time it was not by a shining prince; this time it was by a powerfully charismatic man whose touch she could feel down to her marrow.

And this time she was not grateful.

An abrupt surging anger rose in her, fed by her body's desire and her mind's revolt. She would not — *would not* — be carried away by someone else. This time she'd control her own damn destiny.

It was only partly a conscious decision; Erin's body was acting even before her mind realized what she was doing. And what she was doing was meeting his force with her own. For the first time in her adult life she tapped into the deep well of passions that her red hair hinted at so truly. Always before overwhelmed by someone else's passion, this time she loosed her own.

It was a palpable force as vital and tempestuous as a summer storm, as untamed as a forest fire.

And though another man might have been scorched by that blaze, Matt was delighted. He felt that hidden, guarded part of her rise up to meet him fiercely as she came alive in his arms, felt the heat of this vital woman igniting his own deepest desires.

Instinct demanded a struggle for supremacy, a clash of wills that would allow no winner or loser but simply swallow them both in the conflagration that would change them forever. And the hardest thing Matt had ever done in his life was to back away from that, to chain an instinctive beast howling an intolerable need for its mate.

Matt drew a deep and shuddering breath as he wrenched his lips away, holding her hard against him because he couldn't bear to release her just yet. He looked down into stormy green eyes and felt an exultation that nearly made him laugh aloud. No timid maiden hiding from life — not she! Waiting, perhaps, just waiting for the moment some wise fate had decreed to breathe fire into a woman meant to burn gloriously.

He had seen it — felt it — in her books, that fire. And then, seeing her face, her serene composure, he had found himself captivated by the seeming paradox. It had intrigued him, and meeting Erin here in her aerie had only increased the fascination. Fire within, composure without, there was a self-contained air about her, as though she had shown her inner self once too often and been kicked for it.

Knowing, now, what lay behind that, Matt wondered if Erin herself understood. Did she understand that Stuart Travis's shallow grasping at emotions had never touched her deeply? That because he had overwhelmed her instantly, her own emotions had lain dormant in a kind of bewildered limbo?

Did she understand that the breathless rush she had described had protected her, in a very real sense, from the devastating hurt of love betrayed? Could she see, he wondered, that her "fall" from that prince's charger had been the collapse of a girl's starry dream rather than a woman's shattered love?

Matt could see that so clearly. It had to be that. Stuart Travis had married a girl in love with a shining prince, but that was not the girl Matt wanted for himself. He wanted the woman who had blazed to life in his arms, who had responded with desire and temper, with the wholehearted life force that would never be flung at the feet of a man but would reach out and snatch his heart boldly.

Not a docile princess, but a regal queen.

It would take more than a shotgun to drive him away from her now.

He could see the furious temper in her eyes and, knowing without having to ask why she was mad, grinned down at her quite unconsciously. She knew! Whether she realized it or not, Erin Scott knew the difference between naive girl and vital woman.

Erin all but stamped her foot.

"Damn you!" she gasped for the third — or was it fourth? — time. "I *won't* be rushed again! D'you hear me? Stable your damned charger and slow down!"

Still holding her, very conscious of her fingers threaded through his hair, Matt did laugh aloud. "It takes two," he reminded her, cheerful in spite of his body's fury at obstinate self-control.

Rather hastily, she disentangled her fingers and pushed vainly against his broad chest. Matt laughed again, infuriating man that he was.

"And you thought we could have a simple little affair," he pointed out dryly. He shook his head in gentle disbelief, still easily resisting her attempts to escape him.

Erin stopped struggling and glared up at him. She was absolutely furious, as much at herself as at him. "You listen to me! I'll take control of my own life, dammit! I'll never again be carried along by someone else like some starry-eyed idiot! Never again! I'll *take* this time, I'll *demand* what's mine and won't wait to have it handed to me on a plate like a reward for being a good girl!"

"Good."

The soft, delighted word stopped her abruptly, and she saw bemusedly that Matt really meant it. He *wanted* her to fight for herself, for her fights as a woman.

Matt kissed her briefly, hard, then grinned down at her. "You fight me every inch of the way, wildcat. Yell at me — hit me if you want. Because the passion in you is worth whatever it takes to free itself."

In something like horror, Erin realized then that she had just announced to both of them that there would be no patient, cautious exploration of whatever lay between them. No matter what his intentions were or how strongly she wanted no complications in her life, it seemed a decision had been made. This was something to be fought furiously, emotionally, mastered like a green colt until it could be handled tamely.

"Oh, no," she said numbly. "Not —"

"Don't say *again*," he interrupted instantly. "It wasn't like this before, Erin. What just exploded between us is something I'll bet Stuart Travis would have sold his soul for — if only to write about it. But he never felt what I just felt from you. I don't know why —" Matt hesitated for the first time, then went on. "I don't know why that's so. Maybe you were so overpowered by him, by what you thought he was. Maybe it just wasn't in you then.

"But the point is that it's in you *now*. And I *want* it, Erin! I want that passion. I don't care if I get my fingers burned, or my heart — I want it. If I have to needle you until you strike out at me, kiss you until you fight me,

93

force you to feel it in spite of yourself — I'll get it."

It should have frightened her, Erin thought dimly, his utter determination. But something in her recognized the difference between taking and giving in to his demand; he would take, certainly, but only what he could make her give to him. Only what he could draw from her because she willed it.

She stepped back, and this time he allowed it. But they were still touching, she realized. There was some elusive link between them now, something tying them inexorably together. Something born in a rush of fierce temper and unleashed passion. She could feel the storm of her own temper in her eyes, and his eyes were alight with a satisfaction and anticipation he made no effort to hide.

Erin no longer felt daunted by the thought of violent emotions; instead, she felt curiously energized. She felt as if something long trapped and hidden inside her had burst suddenly into life. "And what," she asked evenly, "am I supposed to get from this?"

"Anything you can take." He smiled slowly. "Whatever you can hold on to. You want me at your feet, Erin? Put me there. You want my heart? Take it. Fight for it. You want to send me tearing back to the city carrying a load of emotional buckshot — fire away."

Staring at him, she said slowly, "I let Stuart use me. I didn't lift a finger to stop him."

Matt nodded. "Now you see it. And now you've got the chance to see if that would happen again. I know it wouldn't; I know that I'd never do that to you, and that you'd never allow it to happen. But you aren't sure of that. So we'll fight it out until you are sure."

"Will we fight — in there?" she asked, nodding toward the bedroom, feeling, with a sense of surprise, no embarrassment at the blunt question.

"We'll fight to get there." He nodded, seeing the comprehension on her face. "It'd be too easy to start there, wouldn't it? Too easy for us. But we will get there — eventually."

"You're very sure of yourself," she muttered, silently acknowledging that he had reason to be. Matt, thankfully, didn't point out the obvious.

"I know what I want," was his only response to that. "But there is something we'd better agree on up front."

"Which is?" she asked warily.

"We have to reach a compromise. Somewhere between your aversion to cities and my ineptitude with wilderness lies a middle ground. We have to find it."

For a moment Erin silently resisted that suggestion. It implied, she knew, a more solid and long-lasting relationship than the one she had had in mind. But she saw the challenge in his eyes and squared her shoulders unconsciously. "All right. But I don't see how to compromise on that. You live in New York, and I live here."

"Ummm." He looked at her for a moment, then said, "We'll have to work on that, I see. And we will. In the meantime, however, I suggest we suspend hostilities in favor of lunch."

Erin started, surprised to realize that it was only just past noon. And then she remembered something else. "Didn't you get in touch with — what's his name? Steve?"

Matt grinned at her. "Sure I did. We had a nice little chat. He's down in town letting kids climb all over Sadie. I told him to come pick me up around five this afternoon."

She glared at him briefly. "Swine. You knew I wouldn't —"

"Well, I was reasonably sure you wouldn't. Lunch?" he added hopefully.

"I ought to let you starve." Erin went into the kitchen and started banging pots, taking a perverse pleasure in the noise. But Matt merely remarked that his sisters always made a hell of a racket in the kitchen when they were irritated at something — or someone — and that it sounded like home to him.

"How many sisters?" Erin asked ruefully, abandoning her noisy temper because he so obviously understood the reasons behind it. Swine that he was.

"Four. Three older, one younger. My father died when I was young, so my mother and sisters pretty much raised me." He grinned as she sent a discerning glance his way. "I won't say I always enjoyed my upbringing, but it did teach me quite a lot about the feminine mind."

"As opposed to the masculine mind?" she inquired politely.

Blandly, he reminded her, "I didn't tell Steve to bring up my stuff, did I?"

Erin turned her back on his grin, uneasily aware of its charm. Damn the man! How on earth could a woman hope to hold her own against that kind of charisma, coupled with what looked like a shrewd understanding of both temperamental writers and women? And with an absolutely *lethal* physical attraction thrown in for good measure?

Thinking back on the day as she lay alone

in bed late that night, Erin decided that she had managed to hold her own. She was still somewhat bewildered by the flare of emotions between her and Matt, but admitted — to herself — a certain excitement in what was clearly going to be a furious exploration of those emotions.

Matt had wasted little time once his intentions had been made clear. With an easy, confident knowledge of women guiding him unerringly, he had hardly waited for lunch to be over before he'd begun needling her about her "retreat" from life.

Erin had never bothered to explain, even to herself, why she had fled so radically from the life she had led during her marriage. From a hectic, public lifestyle to this lonely wilderness was indeed a drastic change, and she found herself looking at it clearly for the first time.

Still, she defended her actions staunchly to him, snapping like a cornered wild thing whenever he got too close — as he inevitably did — to the wounds that had caused that move. Her temper had elated him and surprised her, but neither attempted to damp the flare of emotions.

"Sure you ran — you had reason to run — but why in hell did you run so far?"

"Because I wanted to, dammit!"

"Why? Why here?"

"I wanted to be alone — and *don't* make a crack about bad lines from movies!"

"Thinks she's Garbo," he had mocked mercilessly, then attacked again before her fury could find voice. "So you came up here and put a nice, safe distance between you and everyone else — above the rest of the world, like some bloody ice maiden, daring anyone to touch you —"

"That isn't true!" Erin had tried frantically to control her own temper then — just once.

"Don't you dare freeze up on me!" he had snapped violently.

Erin had snatched up a book and thrown it at him. She'd missed him, and had been so surprised by her own action that she hadn't minded his laughter.

Alone now in the darkness of her bedroom, Erin laughed a little in surprise and bemused amusement. Throwing things, for heaven's sake!

She knew what Matt was doing, of course, because he made absolutely no attempt to disguise his actions. He needled her coolly, openly enjoying her angry responses. He was neither cruel nor unfeeling, but simply determined to wake her up with a vengeance.

When the helicopter had come to retrieve him, he had patted her familiarly on the bottom and grinned unrepentantly at her audible snarl. And when the helicopter had swooped away, Erin had sat down on the steps and laughed without being sure why.

Not, she thought, because her would-be (and probably *soon* would be) lover came courting — or whatever — in a helicopter no self-respecting pilot would have flown and no one else could look at without gasping. Not because of the music that had been, this time, that "godawful marching music."

She laughed, she decided later, at the bewildering turn of events that had deposited a very peculiar prince on her doorstep. His charger was not a galloping white beast, but rather a violent green machine that came and went with a fanfare of music. If he carried a shield, it was cheerful confidence, and his lance was a rather unnerving understanding.

"What're you hiding from, Erin? Him?" Matt had asked.

"No. No, I —"

"Yourself? He shattered your self-confidence, didn't he?"

"I couldn't cope!" she'd admitted at last, fierily.

"He couldn't cope! Stop blaming yourself!"

But she did, in some way, blame herself. It took two to make — or break — a marriage.

And Erin wasn't blinded this time by the brilliance of fantasy. She had a notion that this prince wore his tarnish proudly and openly, counting it as a warrior would count a battle scar: something earned in cheerful pursuit of life. His aim was not to sweep her off her feet, but to rouse in her a strength and willingness to jump aboard his charger freely and with both eyes wide open.

And if nothing else, he certainly woke her up. Erin had been conscious of no limbo, no suspension in her life; she could look back now and see both.

She could also see that Matt had chosen a perfect method to challenge her self-confidence — and capture her heart. She didn't want to think about the latter, but this day had opened up a part of her, and she faced the realization without flinching.

Like Stuart, Matt had come abruptly into her life, showing almost instantly a style and manner she found enormously attractive — but hardly the same style and manner as Stuart's. Where Stuart had been brash and overpowering, Matt had been at first cautious and then, unerringly, challenging. He had not swept her off her feet but had shown her that he *could* — and dared her to stop him.

He didn't draw emotion from her, but goaded her to throw it at him, mocked her mercilessly until she could have strangled him and instead found herself responding with a passion she had never suspected in herself.

She was, she realized staunchly, fascinated by the man. He had come with a weary, beard-stubbled face and eyed her in puzzlement the first day; on the second day he had probed tentatively; and on the third day he had first listened with patience to her and then had quite contentedly gone about rattling the secure — if cowardly — foundations of her life.

Erin was rather amusedly certain that this prince would tuck his crown in a pocket or lay it aside absently because he'd feel ridiculous wearing it; not like Stuart, who had worn his crown with arrogant self-satisfaction. Facing a ten-mile ride up a mountain to see his lady, Stuart would sulk; Matt, finding his charger temperamental, had simply gone looking for the mechanical equivalent. And faced with a stubborn and wary woman, Stuart would have cajoled and charmed; Matt stood back for a measuring look and then waded happily into the fray.

Matt could claim ineptitude with wilderness, but Erin had the shrewd suspicion that he would land on his feet no matter where fate chose to drop him. She wondered then in sudden curiosity if he felt an aversion to her lifestyle, or simply intended to force her to examine it for good points and bad.

And being Erin — this new Erin, who gloried in the straightforward battle they were engaged in — she wasted no time in asking him. And she was in a temper when she asked, because Matt's charger woke her at the crack of dawn the next morning, after a somewhat sleepless night, with its vibrating roar and fanfare of *Bolero*.

Climbing from her bed, she swore steadily and stumbled through the house to wrench open the front door, glaring out on the world in general, and Matt in particular.

Chester, taking an interest today in the music, lifted his muzzle and howled mournfully from behind her. Erin winced, her glare deepening.

"Good morning!" Matt shouted lightheartedly as he reached the steps and Ravel thundered away over the trees.

"Go away!" she shouted back, the final word rather loud since Ravel was fading into the distance.

"Not," Matt said politely, "on your life."

Erin got a grip on herself and the doorjamb. With steely politeness she said, "I do not appreciate being awakened at dawn by that ungodly racket."

"Sorry." Matt responded with no sign of contrition, eyeing her in obvious enjoyment.

Looking down at herself, Erin realized that she was wearing a T-shirt that barely covered the tops of her thighs. With nothing underneath it. Refusing to be embarrassed, she looked him fiercely in the eye. "Gentlemen," she told him, "don't come calling at dawn!"

"I'm not a gentleman, I'm a general. And an army marches on its stomach. How about breakfast?" Stepping onto the porch, he continued to gaze at her appreciatively, with a definite gleam in his eye. "Tell you what — I'll cook. You can just stand around looking seductive in that outfit." Thoughtfully, he added, "I'll burn everything, but what the hell."

Erin ignored the laugh that was trying to choke her. "You're an impossible man!" The accusation lost something of its force, since she had to step back into the cabin as he advanced.

Chester lifted his lip at the visitor, and it got stuck on his upper teeth. He sat there, seemingly glaring at both of them but managing to look surprised. Helpfully, Matt reached down to smooth the wrinkle and hide a few gleaming canine incisors. Chester thumped his tail once in gratitude or perhaps acknowledgment. Matt patted him on the head in a friendly manner.

Erin got a grip on herself and fought an inner battle to keep laughter at bay. Crossing her arms beneath her breasts in an unconsciously provocative gesture, she demanded intensely, "D'you hate my lifestyle?"

Addressing the cleavage visible at the V neckline of her sleepshirt, Matt said absently, "What? Oh, no, of course not." After a long silence, he lifted his gaze and grinned a bit sheepishly. "Well, dammit, Erin —"

"Lecher!" she accused him somewhat breathlessly. Grin or not, there was something very male in his eyes, and it affected her strongly.

Assuming an expression of extreme patience, Matt said, "My darling Erin, I can hardly walk and talk at the same time around you. If I manage not to stutter, it's only because I'm not prone to it. In case you're interested, my heart's doing flips like a landed fish, and my pulse rate and blood pressure would probably put me in a hospital if a doctor were around to measure them."

Erin uncrossed her arms and cleared her

throat, wondering what in the world she could say to that. Luckily, Matt wasn't waiting to find out.

"I came up here this early because I couldn't sleep, and Steve brought me happily because he always gets up with the chickens. And since it's your fault that I couldn't sleep, I decided to wake you up. Although," he added musingly, eyeing her, "I never expected such a nice reward."

Erin wanted to lift a lip at him in an adaptation of Chester's snarl, but found herself giggling instead. "You sound like a besotted adolescent!" she exclaimed, choking.

"I'll probably start to drool in a minute," he agreed amiably. Then added in a different tone, "For godsake, Erin, go get dressed before I carry you and the battle into the bedroom."

The fact that she obeyed this command, Erin decided moments later as she pulled a sweater over her head, had nothing to do with docility. It was, she acknowledged ruefully, more along the lines of discretion being the better part of valor. She brushed her hair, debated briefly, left it down.

Pausing before leaving her bedroom, Erin studied herself in the mirror. She was, in a sense, perversely armed for battle. Her jeans were tight, molding hips and legs lovingly.

Her sweater boasted a V neckline far deeper than the sleepshirt, and was a soft coral that made the visible flesh warmly pale and added an extra gleam to her hair and eyes. Or maybe, she thought in sudden amusement, the glint in her eyes owed nothing to the sweater.

Girded for battle, Erin strolled out of her bedroom and stood near the breakfast bar, gazing at Matt. He was working busily, whistling between his teeth. Pancakes, from the look of it, she thought, watching him expertly mixing ingredients.

"I'm going to feed the horses," she announced.

Matt glanced over his shoulder with "okay" forming on his lips — but only the first letter and sound made it. He stood there with a whisk in one hand, the other gripping a large mixing bowl . . . and managed to look amazingly masculine. He took an unwary step toward her, trod on Chester's tail, and jumped at the yelp.

"Sorry, Chester," he said automatically.

Erin smiled in a gentle manner and turned toward the back door.

Matt found himself leaning back to look around the bar and watch her, caught himself, and swore softly. He concentrated on mixing the batter, wondering if his ears were red. Probably, he decided; they felt hot. *He* felt hot.

He was grinning a little. Did she, he wondered, realize just how true his earlier words had been? Never one to hide from himself, Matt acknowledged silently that if he hadn't stuttered in her presence, it was only because he'd managed to straighten out his tongue at the last possible second. And just because he hadn't tripped over his own feet didn't mean it couldn't happen at any time now.

God, she was lovely! Caged fire. He felt like an adolescent around her, forced to constantly remind himself he was a grown man, dammit, and could keep his hands to himself. But every time he looked at her he felt a jolting shock that took away his breath and made him dizzy.

She was more beautiful with each glance, more desirable, more everything. Even half asleep and mad as hell as she greeted him — violently — at the door, she'd caused tension to coil in his stomach and heat to burn through him.

He was still astonished that he hadn't attacked her with a primeval howl and gnashing teeth.

Ruefully, he decided not to congratulate himself on his restraint just yet. She was, obviously, carrying the battle into treacherous territory; the vixen had worn that sweater with malice aforethought.

It gave him hope, though, that sweater. In addition to a near heart attack. It gave him hope because it stated plainly her lack of fear in consequences. She was, he decided, waving her red cape at the bull with full knowledge of the creature's horns.

At least . . . he hoped so.

He felt rather like pawing the ground.

Matt managed to keep his boots still when she returned. He even managed to hold a semi-intelligent conversation over breakfast.

"Could you pass the butter, please?"

"Certainly."

"Thank you."

"You're welcome."

"Chester, stop chewing on my ankle. Does he want a pancake?"

"He probably wants a beer."

"I beg your pardon?"

"He's a recovering alcoholic. Don't give him any firewater."

Matt leaned back to gaze down at the unnatural animal sharpening his teeth on his leather boot. "Um. Right." He welcomed the distraction of Chester's peculiarities, since every glance at Erin glued his tongue to the roof of his mouth. But then she twisted on the barstool to look down at her dog, and Matt choked on his coffee.

"Go down the wrong way?" she asked sympathetically.

Wiping streaming eyes, Matt looked for a gleam in hers and found only mild concern. He fought the urge to lunge and said, "Um."

"I'll clean up," she said a few moments later. "You cooked. And very well, too."

"Thanks." He didn't offer to help, not sure he could get off the barstool without making a fool of himself. He propped an elbow on the bar, drinking coffee and smoking a cigarette, barely feeling Chester's continued munching.

Matt watched her move about the kitchen and tried reciting the multiplication tables silently. When that failed him, he dredged his mind for every impossibly corny love poem he could recall.

He would, he decided, have to make her mad again. At least when she was yelling at him he could chain that part of him bent on lunging.

Maybe.

He was, after all, a grown man.

Chapter Five

Matt was finishing his third cup of coffee when Erin turned to look at him, a little puzzled, a little amused. "Are you wedded to that barstool?"

He thought about it, answered, "No." Then he managed to get off the barstool without falling over his own feet. The accomplishment was mildly pleasing to him. "Eve must have looked like that," he observed.

"Like what?"

"Amused." Matt sighed. "I don't think we've learned a damn thing since Adam chased Eve through the garden."

"What are we talking about?" Erin asked.

Matt resisted an urge to get on all fours and howl, reminding himself that men walked like men, dammit. "I," he said, "am talking about a siren let loose in my garden. Can we go outside? I need some air."

Erin followed as he bolted (Matt couldn't think of another word for it) out the front door.

"Claustrophobia?" she asked, still honestly bewildered.

Matt looked down to find that Chester had also followed and was now chewing on the other boot. He sighed. Then he looked at Erin, which was a mistake. The morning sun made her hair gleam like copper and her skin like fine porcelain.

There was, Matt decided calmly, a limit to patience. He nudged Chester aside, stepped toward Erin, and allowed his instincts a modified lunge.

"Not claustrophobia," he said in a voice Chester might have claimed for a growl. "A siren."

This time Erin felt no conscious urging to fight his fire with her own — she simply and instinctively did so. Her body felt hot, liquid, molding itself to his with a sense of affinity too strong to resist. Her knees went weak and her lips responded to his as if they had been created just for that reason, that response. There was no way she could have pulled back.

But Matt, with too much at stake, could pull back. He didn't want to, and God knew it was almost impossible to do so . . . but he did it. Barely.

By the time he came up for air, Erin needed it. She stared up at him, a bit dazed, a little surprised because he had seemed so calm and cheerful in spite of his earlier claim of a fast pulse and high blood pressure. She wasn't at all surprised, though, to find her arms around his lean waist.

"Release me, madam," Matt ordered somewhat hoarsely, "or I'll ravish you."

Erin felt a heart pounding and wasn't sure if it was hers or his. With an effort she managed to release him and step back.

"I hate rejection," Matt told Chester. Chester growled sympathetically.

"You told me —" she began indignantly.

"Do you always do what you're told?" he demanded, being quite fierce about it.

Unaware that her reasoning was the same as his, Erin decided to resume the argument of the day before. "Look, if you don't hate my lifestyle, why're you so scornful of it?"

Matt blinked, adjusted his mind rather hastily, and waved a hand at the lonely grandeur surrounding them. "This is a fine place to come to," he said firmly, "but a bad place to *run* to. And three years is too damn long to hide up here."

"I'm not hiding!"

"No?" Matt slid his hands into his pockets to hide the stray tremor and rocked back on his heels. "Prove it."

"How?"

"Spend the day with me tomorrow in Denver. Steve'll fly us, and we'll lose ourselves in the city." He paused, adding blandly, "And see a concert tomorrow night."

Erin, on the point of accepting the dare, hesitated and felt suspicious. "Concert?"

"Uh-huh." Matt lifted a gentle brow and related a piece of information he'd discovered the day before. "Stuart Travis."

"You — swine!" Erin said when she could.

Satisfied with the reaction that was anger rather than fear or pain, Matt nodded firmly. "I'll box shadows, Erin. I'll even punch out flesh and blood. But I want to be sure of what I'm fighting. And I want you to take a good long look at what you ran away from."

Erin stared at him. "Fine!" she snapped. "I'll go to Denver, I'll go to the damned concert. But right now I'm going riding!"

Matt stepped off the porch when she did. "Good. So will I."

"You can't ride," she reminded him, annoyed.

"Then you'll just have to teach me, won't you?"

Erin made a sound that might have been a snort if it hadn't come from a lady, and she headed for the barn.

Looking at the clean, defiant line of her slender back, Matt nearly tripped, and swore inwardly. Walking behind her for reasons he didn't have to think about, he blocked a wistful sound at the back of his throat and concentrated on walking like a man.

It didn't seem to get any easier.

Erin saddled both horses, her temper easing so that she could explain to Matt how horses were saddled and tell him the basics of handling the animals. Such as to beware of sharp teeth.

"Hell!" he yelped, jumping aside as the gray, Tucker, attempted to bite him.

"He bites," she explained, not without a certain pleasure.

Looking at the horse he'd ridden down the mountain the day after he'd found Erin, and which he was holding by the bridle, Matt said, "This one doesn't, huh?"

"Amos? No, he's sweet-tempered. Easy to ride. Tucker, on the other hand, is a mass of bad habits." Tightening the girth, she briskly brought one knee up against the gelding's side, and he released air in an indignant snort. "He holds his breath," she said, quickly tightening the girth an extra couple of inches.

"That's bad?" Matt wouldn't have thought a horse's personal habits were of any concern to humans.

Erin gave him a patient look. "It is if

you're planning to keep a saddle on his back. They aren't put on with glue, you notice."

Matt chuckled a little at the tolerance in her voice.

"All right, so I'm ignorant. Willing, though." He led his own mount from the barn behind hers, carefully keeping his distance from Tucker's heels; he didn't need to be told that *that* end was dangerous.

Erin gathered the reins and said, "Don't mount up yet. Tucker usually fights me. Stay put until he settles down."

Before Matt could say a word, she swung up on the horse. On the fury, he amended almost instantly, his heart leaping into his throat as the gray animal instantly gave his imitation of a rodeo bronc — and it was a fine imitation. It was, in fact, an award-winning performance. He bucked wildly, snorting, lunging, whirling in a mad circle. He tried fiercely to get his head down between his knees to buck harder, frustrated by Erin's expert hand on the reins. He tried even more furiously to get her off his back, twice nearly going over backward in the attempt.

Matt knew — he *knew* — that Erin was a horsewoman. He knew she was safe, that the horse wouldn't hurt her. But his heart pounded sickly in his chest, and he felt cold with fear. He gripped Amos's reins with white-knuckled fingers, rooted to the ground. And even through his dread he felt a surge of emotions that had nothing to do with fear.

She rode like a Valkyrie, seemingly a part of the furious beast who fought her. Her copper hair flew wildly, and her face, her lovely face, was curiously intent in a kind of elemental pleasure. With grace and skill and determination she mastered half a ton of enraged animal, and the barbaric beauty of the contest was breathtaking.

And then, suddenly, it was over. Tucker stood very still and stiff for a moment, then let out his breath in a snort and stamped one hoof in what was clearly irritation. Then he relaxed and yawned.

Erin, a little flushed but calm, glanced over at Matt. "He's finished," she said. "Ready to go?"

"You'll get indigestion riding like that so soon after breakfast," Matt said. It sounded like a croak to him, but Erin seemed to notice nothing.

"I'm fine. Mount up."

Matt got into the saddle, noticing absently that the imprint of the reins lay whitely across his palm. He felt decidedly precarious on his horse, wondering with something between bewilderment and admiration how Erin managed to look so damned *at home* on hers.

They started along a trail that wound away behind the barn, able to walk side by side. Still conscious of his pounding heart, Matt cleared his throat.

"Why in God's name do you keep that hellion?" he asked.

She looked faintly surprised. "Nothing's perfect, Matt. Tucker has excellent gaits, and he'll go anywhere I ask once he resigns himself to a rider."

Matt shook his head on an instinctive thought. "It isn't just that, though. You *like* the fight."

Erin frowned a little, clearly dealing with something new. "I suppose," she said slowly. "I never really thought about it. I've had Tucker since I came up here, and he fights me every time I saddle him. Oddly enough, he'll carry a pack with no trouble and no fuss."

"Maybe he enjoys the fight, too."

She reached down to stroke the gray neck that was only slightly damp with the sweat of exertion, and smiled suddenly. "Maybe you're right."

Matt knew he was right. She and the

horse fought, neither of them willing to submit. But the horse submitted first. Perhaps it was a point of equine honor with Tucker to fight; Matt thought it was something deeper and more basic with Erin.

Caged fire.

They rode companionably for nearly two hours, taking various trails that wound up and down the mountainous terrain, talking idly when they rode side by side and falling silent when the trail forced them to go single file. Chester accompanied them, going off on his own occasionally and then returning to make certain they weren't lost — or at least that was the impression he gave.

Erin watched Matt without, she trusted, being obvious about it. She was impressed by his grace and ease in the saddle, knowing very well that he was unaccustomed to horses or riding. Still, he rode well and handled his horse with a firm hand.

She had always thought that riding a horse brought out the best or worst in the human body, revealing it as either impossibly awkward or else beautifully fluid; Matt looked strong and lithe, with a sense of restrained power.

And he seemed attuned to the beauty of nature, watching everything but commenting only with a quick smile or an intentness in his gray eyes.

He guided Amos to follow or walk beside Tucker across streams and along narrow cliff-hugging paths, never complaining of an uncomfortable ride or suggesting an easier way. There was no bravado in him; she could neither see nor sense an attitude of the macho I'll-do-it-if-it-kills-me. Thinking again of his adaptability, wondering at it, Erin at last turned them back toward the cabin.

Matt had enjoyed the ride. He still felt precarious on horseback, and some of Erin's decisions as to the proper trail to take had sorely tried what he chose to call his courage. He would, he knew, be painfully aware of the ride for hours — if not days — and wondered if he would ever be able to walk without *looking* as if he'd just gotten off a horse.

The beauty of the place was beginning to affect him. He could better understand now why Erin chose to call it home. But he was, at heart, a creature of the city, and knew that even the lovely wilderness would begin to pall if not for her beside him.

Back at the barn, he dismounted, hoping he didn't look as stiff as he felt, and began unsaddling Amos rather gingerly. Glancing over his shoulder to where Erin briskly unsaddled Tucker, he said idly, "It is a lovely place. I'm surprised no one has thrown up a resort hotel or something."

"I wouldn't let that happen," she responded absently, carrying Tucker's saddle into the small tack room.

Matt followed with the second saddle. "You wouldn't?" He felt a little startled.

She looked surprised herself, then sighed. "When I came back here, Matt, I came home in a way. My grandmother used to live in the cabin. She owned the mountain. Now it's mine."

He thought about that while they groomed the horses and stabled them, not commenting until they'd returned to the cabin and carried coffee out to the porch.

"No one told me you owned the mountain," he ventured finally.

Erin, leaning back against one of the support posts and sipping her coffee, watched him light a cigarette, and shrugged. "People around here mind their own business."

Matt leaned against the post on the opposite side of the steps, gazing at her quietly. "Did you live up here while you were growing up?"

"No. Visited sometimes, but not often. My parents preferred the city. Still do. I grew up in Los Angeles."

Neutrally, he asked, "School?"

"Stanford," she answered briefly.

"I went to William and Mary. Grew up in D.C."

Erin shook her head a little, smiling. "See how incompatible we are? Me from California — an unconventional state, if nothing else. You from the traditional East."

Matt smiled in return, a smile that was a little wry and a little amused, as if he could have disagreed with her. But all he said was, "We're meeting on fairly neutral ground. And we've both seen more of life than childhood. I don't think our backgrounds will come between us."

She stared into her coffee cup for a moment, then set it aside. She looked at him. "I'm not hiding."

"That rankled," he noted dryly.

"Of course it rankled. Nobody likes to be called a coward. All right — I was hiding when I came. But not now. Not for a long time now."

"As long as you know that."

After a minute Erin said, "Damn you."

Matt grinned faintly. "You didn't know, did you? You weren't sure. But after you had to defend your choice, you did know." He watched her, watched her think about that. Watched her smile and felt his toes curl.

And he wondered if he would ever grow accustomed to this reaction to her that was physical but emotional and intellectual as well. Somehow, he didn't think he would. Not in this lifetime.

She saluted him with an inclination of her head. "All right, General — that's one point for your side. What do we fight about next?"

"Are you writing?"

She stirred, uneasy. "No. I don't feel like working."

"Maybe," he suggested neutrally, "you're ready for a change in your life. Less — peace and quiet?"

Erin frowned a little. "I just don't feel like writing. I need a break, that's all."

"All right," he responded easily.

She was silent for a while, wondering what he was thinking. Unnervingly, he seemed to pick up the mental question and answered it with a flickering smile.

"Tight sweaters," he murmured.

"Yours or mine?" she asked, deadpan, managing to hide her inward start of surprise.

Matt looked down rather pointedly at his flannel shirt, then lifted a brow at her. "I'm not wearing one. If it'll cause you to feel a faint pang of lust, I'll get rid of what I do have, though."

"Wouldn't want you to catch cold."

"And it wouldn't spark an interest in my manly body anyway, huh?"

"Don't fish."

Matt brooded at her. "Maybe I'll bring ravishing maidens back into style."

"Will you pillage too?"

"Desperately."

They both watched impassively as Chester climbed onto the porch and collapsed between them. He sat up abruptly as though remembering something, scratched fiercely behind his left ear, then lay down again with a contented sigh.

Matt looked at Erin. "A recovering alcoholic?"

"Yes."

He wished he could think of further conversation regarding Chester. It was, he'd decided, far safer to stare at a mutant grizzly bear than at a redheaded Erin. But certainly more fun to stare at Erin. Even if it hurt.

"You look," she observed dispassionately, "as if you were starved for sweets and someone had closed the doughnut shop in your face."

He started laughing, shaking his head when she looked quizzical. "Never mind. Maybe it's the mountain air, but I'm already hungry again. Why don't we pack a picnic lunch and go find a spectacular view?"

Erin decided not to question. She merely agreed and went inside the cabin with him. She wondered more than once during the following hour why she couldn't seem to breathe whenever he was close, ignoring all the instincts that were telling her why.

She caught herself watching him beneath her lashes, watching strong hands move with grace. Watching shoulders that were wide and powerful. Watching, obliquely, a face that was very handsome and very masculine.

She listened to his voice, responding automatically to words she hardly heard, meeting his smiling eyes occasionally, her own skittering away. Fighting was one thing, she decided, but becoming a kamikaze was something else entirely.

She hadn't been able to cope with Stuart's demands on her, and a part of her was still uneasy about coping with this new relationship. He could hurt her, she knew. Hurt her more unbearably than Stuart had. If she lost anything to Matt, it would not be a dream. It would be a part of herself.

She wondered if moths knew flames would destroy them, and went on in spite of knowledge.

She thought they did.

★ ★ ★

They carried a picnic basket and blanket farther up the mountain, at last reaching Erin's favorite place. The trail ended abruptly at the edge of the cliff, a spectacular view framed by the deep green of pine trees, like a picture of raw beauty. They looked down on the valley far below, at tiny dollhouses and minute roads. And when they looked straight out from the cliff, mountains shouldered one another in sharp angles and arrogant peaks, closer to the sky than anything man could carve from the ground.

They spread the bright yellow blanket on a layer of pine needles that promised softness and just enjoyed the view for a long time in companionable silence.

Later, while they rapidly disposed of the satisfying lunch, Erin looked at her glass of wine and felt guilty.

They had left Chester in the cabin entirely against his will — he'd seen the bottle — and he had let them know in no uncertain terms how unhappy he was about the situation.

Unerringly reading her expression, Matt grinned and said, "I wonder if he's still howling."

"Probably," Erin said wryly. "He won't be destructive because we shut him up in the cabin, but he'll sulk for the rest of the day."

"How in the world did he — ?"

"Stuart's idea of something funny. It wouldn't have mattered if Chester hadn't liked the taste. But he did, and — Oh, well. I went back to the house once when I knew Stuart was on the road, and I stole Chester," she added abruptly. "He really belonged to Stuart."

They were silent for a while. The remains of lunch were packed neatly away, leaving only the wine they sipped.

Finally, as abruptly as she had spoken before, Matt said, "Did it hurt so badly?"

Erin, lying on her stomach only a few safe feet from the cliff edge, nodded slowly without looking at him. "It did then. Oh, not the other woman. Oddly enough, that barely hurt at all. But the rest of it. The feeling my life was no longer mine. The understanding that . . . that Stuart had taken what I was, what we were, and turned us into songs people sung with their radios."

She pushed away her empty wineglass and rolled onto her back, staring up at the ceiling of green needles. "Cheap," she said curtly. "It cheapened me, what I felt. Or thought I felt. Maybe another woman could have coped. I couldn't." Her sigh was a soft rush of sound. "I was in the studio when he recorded that song. The one about his new love. He looked at me while he sang. Oh, he didn't mean to be cruel; Stuart never meant to be cruel. He was just explaining the only way he knew how. He looked surprised when I walked out."

After a moment she turned her head and looked at Matt, wondering vaguely what went on behind his immobile expression. "A few months after the divorce, I was in town and heard his latest song on the radio." She smiled a small, wry smile. "It was about the death of love — and a marriage. The music industry gave him three awards for it."

Matt sat with his back against a tree and gazed at her, telling himself that she had hurt because a dream had died — not love. He didn't want to think that she had known love and that some other man had killed it.

He moved suddenly until he was lying beside her, raised on an elbow to look down at her. "He couldn't touch the passion in you," Matt said softly. "He couldn't destroy that. He killed a girl's dream, Erin . . . not a woman's love."

She stared up at him. *"You want my heart? Fight for it."* With a shock she could feel all through her body, Erin realized then that she did want his heart. And that this was no wistful yearning for the heart of an elusive comet; this was a compulsive need, a desperate hunger for a strong heart she would have fought for had it lain inside hell's gates.

"Fight for it."

Erin fought the only way she knew.

She was reaching up even as he leaned toward her, seeing in his flaring eyes the reflection of her own, seeing a face she hardly knew because it seemed transformed by a sudden and terrible need. A slumbering fire ignited instantly when his lips captured hers . . . or hers took him captive.

Erin felt the rough flannel beneath her fingers and, beneath that, the hard power of muscles and sinew and bone, of flesh and blood too real to ever be a dream shattered by a song. She felt the seeking demand of warm, hard lips, the primitive possession of wine-sweet breath moving hotly from his mouth to hers. The heavy weight of him lay half over her, his heart thudding like a living thing caged against her. His thick, silky hair was tangled between her fingers, and his belt buckle dug into her hip with the sharpness of reality.

A strong hand slipped beneath her back, beneath the sweater to touch and inflame like a brand. Her breasts were crushed against his chest, throbbing in a sweet near-pain, trapped by clothing, aching for his touch.

Again and again he kissed her, deep, drugging kisses that sapped her strength and her soul. But the force of her, the elemental power so recently freed she willingly gave him, her response as fiery, as strong and hungry as his own desire. Everything that she was leaned toward him as a flower to the sun.

His lips traced the line of her jaw, her throat, her forehead, leaving behind them a trail of stinging awareness. His hand slid around to lie warmly against her stomach while his free hand tangled in her long hair.

"Erin . . . dear God . . ." He caught his breath on a ragged sound when her own hand found the smooth, tanned skin of his back, traced his spine with caressing fingers. With her nails she scratched lightly, feeling him tremble, and his lips were hot and shaking against her throat.

Matt could barely breathe, feeling his heart pounding like a runaway engine in his chest. Her every touch made him that much more hungry, that much more desperate for her. Rational thought sank like a stone beneath the overpowering weight of fierce desire. He wanted her so badly that nothing else mattered; nothing else could be felt except the aching demand within him to know her completely.

Nothing else mattered.

She heard a faint whimper, knowing only vaguely that the sound came from her, from somewhere deep inside her, where hunger coiled and writhed and tension gathered like anguish.

She whispered his name, unable to find her voice or her breath or any will at all except the will to have this go on forever, past the point of pain and far beyond thought. Her lithe body, made strong by the work of wilderness, arched of its own accord to press against his. Her arms held him tightly, and her thigh quivered at the hard power of the desire it pressed against.

"Erin," he murmured. "Erin . . ." His hand stroked her stomach, the silky flesh beneath his touch vibrating with tremors of need. The pulse in her throat beat frantically like the wings of a small bird under his lips, and the soft sounds she made ran like fire through his veins.

On some dim and distant level of his mind, Matt knew they were fighting still, fighting as men and women had always fought. Man and woman, eternally different, eternally destined to join in spite of differences and because of them. Destined to strike sparks off one another's souls in a clash taking them very nearly to death.

But he knew something else as well, something he tried desperately to ignore because molten heat flowed through his aching body, and his need for her tortured him. He fought the knowledge for eternal moments, for heartbeats, his senses flaring with the touch of her, the taste of her, the sounds of her desire in his ears.

He wondered if one could die of passion, and thought that here, at least, and now, one could. He could. He didn't think he'd mind dying very much if that were the cost of loving her.

Loving her . . .

The knowledge, the certainty formed, made sense in his mind. And along with that knowledge came the other certainty, the other knowledge he silently damned.

Loving her as he did, he could not make love to her. Not yet. Not with so much still unresolved. They couldn't take the easy way.

With a wrenched groan he rolled away from her, covering his eyes with a forearm and fighting for control of that howling beast. Instinct made him reach out swiftly with his free hand, catching hers and holding it hard to ease the uncomprehending pain of rejection.

Erin lay in silence for a long tense moment, staring upward at the canopy of green pines and feeling bereft, torn. Then she felt the slight pain of his tight grip, and that other pain lessened. She turned finally on her side to face him, holding his hand as tightly as he held hers. She brought her other hand up slowly, enclosing his in both.

His face was half hidden from her, but the white tautness of what she saw both reassured her — and awed her. What was this between them, she pondered, this raw, wild thing that could make of them something they had never been before?

Something *she* had never been before. She didn't think she could bear it if this was something he knew well, had known often. She didn't think it was possible.

He had said — what? That he had never been in love. Was this, then, love? If it was — if it was, she thought, then she had never loved. What she had called love before today seemed a pale and sad thing, a weak and shallow thing.

And that other prince, that bright and shining prince of no substance, faded away almost to nothing, without pain or regret, lost in the shadow of flesh and blood and bone and sinew. And the girl who had fallen off a charger picked herself up and waited with the patience of something deep and sure for the ride that would last forever.

Matt spoke at last without uncovering his eyes, his voice hoarse. "You have to face him. Tomorrow. Put him behind you. Then we go on."

Erin thought about that for a moment, understanding the need for certainty, for resolution. That other prince was gone, but there had been a man as well, and he was still a shadowy, elusive part of her. She had to see that man without the shining armor she had encased him in.

"All right," she said, hardly recognizing the soft, husky sound of her own voice.

"I'll be with you," Matt said. "I won't let you go. Even if he fights for you."

"He won't," she said, knowing that.

"I would." Matt drew a deep harsh breath. "Lord, I would. Erin —"

She brought his hand to her cheek as he turned at last to face her with bright, intense eyes. Before he could follow the choked sound of her name, she said, "After tomorrow. We'll go on after tomorrow."

He nodded slowly, very conscious of what he had nearly said. He didn't know, even now, what it would lead to. He only knew with certainty the depth of his own feelings, the incredulous astonishment he felt in looking at her.

The thorns were still there, of course. And

even now he knew that Erin's meeting with her ex-husband would determine the future of their relationship. Even now. Even if Erin were no longer blinded by shining armor, she could find the man beneath to be too much a part of her to abandon easily — or at all.

And even if she would feel nothing for the man, Matt understood her too well to think that everything would be easy now.

There were still the thorns.

Chapter Six

Erin found she couldn't stop watching him. Just looking at him gave her a pleasure that was nearly painful, and kept hunger rumbling with soft insistence deep inside her. An inner voice impossible to ignore.

The fiery passion he had aroused in her was banked now, and with clear thought came wariness. She had been at the mercy of her feelings once before, and even though every beat of her heart told her this was different, this was real, she was nonetheless frightened.

And Matt knew.

He caught her hand firmly as they walked back down the trail to the cabin, the picnic basket swinging from his freehand. "Tell me, Erin."

After a moment, staring ahead because looking at him weakened her knees and her judgment, she responded slowly. "Back there . . . I was swept away. Nothing mattered." She felt heat in her face, painfully aware that she was handing him a powerful weapon — one an unscrupulous man wouldn't hesitate to use. She felt his gaze and cleared her throat strongly.

"I don't know . . . I can't be sure that I feel what I think I feel . . . I mean — it's happened so damn *fast!*"

"The way it did before?"

She glanced at him, unable to judge from the neutral tone how he might feel about that. His face told her nothing, and she sighed and looked ahead again. "Matt, does it bother you that I can't help comparing?"

"I'd be a liar," he said dryly, "if I said no. At the same time, I understand why you have to. I realize how difficult it is for you, Erin. You were swept off your feet by him, and when you woke up to what was happening, it was to find the whole world staring at you. Then, when you'd finally found peace, I dropped into your life."

He stopped walking and turned to face her, his expression serious. "It's happened fast," he agreed quietly. "We're still strangers, you and I. But we have something, Erin. And whatever it is, it's worth fighting for. So if you have to compare me with him because it helps you to understand, then I can take it. I have to take it. I don't have any choice."

Erin swallowed. "A year isn't very long — but he was all my life during that year. And there was nobody before him. Whatever else he was, he was my husband. And vows *mean* something to me. I thought we were forever." She drew a deep breath. "But it ended. There's nothing between us now but memories. I'm through with him, Matt."

Rather abruptly, Matt started them toward the cabin again. "I wonder if he's through with you . . ."

It was little more than a murmur, and Erin wasn't entirely sure she had heard the words clearly. She felt an inner bitterness that Stuart still had the power to shadow her life, and wondered if facing him now would do any good at all.

Self-doubt and uncertainty crowded into her mind. Could she trust herself not to make the same mistakes again? In the blaze of the incredible passion between her and Matt, could she find enough strength to keep control of her life? Or had Stuart somehow influenced her perception of emotions, teaching her subconsciously that there was only a wild roller-coaster ride with nothing at the end of it but memories?

"You think too much," Matt said suddenly.

"Oh, no! Before, I —" She broke off.

Matt seemed unperturbed by the intended comparison. "You didn't think enough? Probably not. He didn't give you time to think. And now you're going overboard in the other direction, worrying about everything. Well, we both knew we wouldn't take the easy way, didn't we?"

"The easy way." She looked down at their clasped hands. "Physical being less complicated than emotional?"

He smiled a little, but didn't look at her. "Isn't it? We could just follow our urges; I'm having a hell of a time fighting mine."

"Is — that a suggestion?" she asked, wondering if he had changed his mind.

"No, just an observation. I don't know if I'm right in thinking that *would* be the easy way for us, Erin." As they came out of the trees and faced the cabin, he stopped, staring at the neat home as if it represented something more than it was. Then he looked down at her.

"All I do know is that what I want and need from you isn't simple physical passion. And for you to give me what I need requires a trust we don't have yet."

"What do you need?" she asked softly.

"Your love," he answered simply. "Given freely. I don't want the blind worship of a girl for a prince, Erin; I want the love of a woman for a man. I want you to trust me because you see me clearly — in all my human imperfection. No prince in shining armor. Not even a knight. Just a man."

"I'm human, too," she said shakily, then swallowed hard. "And imperfect, Lord knows. It's just — you don't know it all, Matt. It's hard to trust myself not to let it happen again." Blindly, she pulled free of his gentle grasp and went quickly to the cabin. She went inside, leaving the door open and noticing only vaguely that Chester lay by the hearth with his back firmly turned to her. He didn't stir.

Sulking, of course.

Feeling exhausted, drained emotionally and still tautly aware of unsatisfied desire, Erin sank down on the couch and stared down at the hands clasped in her lap. She felt his weight beside her but not touching, and all her nerves shrieked awareness.

"Erin —"

Quickly, softly, aching with a pain that had never entirely left her, she said, "I'd never before lost anything or anyone that mattered, Matt. Never. I guess I led a charmed life; tragedy was something that happened to other people. I knew — intellectually — that death followed life; I never had to deal with the death of anyone I knew personally. The odds are against it, I suppose. In more than twenty years of living, one usually has to face death and loss. But I never did."

Matt shifted a bit on the couch, and his arm lifted to lay across the low back. His hand moved to grasp her shoulder very gently. "I see."

She knew that he didn't see, couldn't possibly know. But he had to know. She had to tell him, because her marriage had shaped so much of what she was. They both had to face that.

"Matt . . . it wasn't the end of a marriage or the death of — of a dream that caused me to run up here and hide. Those were . . . final blows, but they broke me only because any blow would have broken me then."

"Something else happened," he said slowly.

Erin nodded blindly, feeling suddenly the welling of grief that had never been allowed to escape in a normal and healthy release, grief that had lain deeply buried in her for more than three years, alone in the darkness. It was a primitive, soul-deep emotion, and it had torn her up inside.

"Tell me," Matt urged quietly.

"I'd never lost anyone before." She was talking more to herself than to him, reliving the shock and pain, the fear and horror of abruptly facing the fragility of life. "But I lost him. He moved inside me for months and then . . . I just lost him. If I could have held on to him for one more month, they could have saved him."

The hand on her shoulder tightened suddenly, convulsively, and Matt's deep voice was unsteady with anguish. "You lost your baby? Oh, Erin — I'm sorry!"

Her eyes filled with hot tears that spilled free to run down her cheeks. His had been an instant and honest expression of sympathy for a real and devastating loss. Such simple words. But Stuart hadn't been able to say them.

To him it had meant only a minor inconvenience, a bad dress rehearsal before the real performance.

"Don't look so stricken, honey. We'll have another kid. The doc says they're letting you out of here in a few days, so you can meet me in Detroit. I have to catch the jet this afternoon. You need anything before I go? No? See you in Detroit then, baby."

Erin felt strong arms drawing her close, and she hid her face against Matt's warm throat. She didn't sob, but her voice was jerky, and the tears flowed as though released from a dam.

"He didn't *care!* He never even said he was sorry. And he'd acted excited about the

baby." She laughed, and it was a terrible
sound. "A baby was something new, you
see. He'd never been a father before. He
wanted to — experience it. He was even going to take childbirth instructions, because
he wanted to be there. But then I miscar-
ried. And he — he didn't even say he was
sorry. The baby wasn't *real* to him. He felt it
kick in me — but *he wasn't sorry it died!*"

And then she cried.

Matt held her tightly, stroking her hair but
making no attempt to halt her difficult,
rasping sobs. Held her and wondered savagely what kind of bastard could feel no
pain at the death of his child.

He didn't even have to imagine how he
would feel himself. He loved children, and
had often abandoned office and work to
baby-sit for his sisters when they'd come to
New York on visits; between his four sisters
he had three nephews and four nieces rang-
ing in age from two to nineteen, and every
one had discovered as toddlers that their
uncle was the world's softest touch.

He had paced the floor with more than
one brother-in-law, and had once disrupted
airline schedules by pulling every string he
could find in order to get to the West Coast
in the middle of the night because his
younger sister had come frighteningly close

to losing her first child.

He held Erin even more tightly, aching for her pain and grief, feeling a savage anger that any man had hurt her like that. A dream shattered had hurt, certainly, but it was nothing compared to the devastation of losing a child.

And at a moment when her husband should have held her, grieved with her, he had instead dismissed months of life and an agonizing loss with a callous insensitivity.

Matt had never considered himself a violent man, but he knew that if Stuart Travis had stood before him right then, he would have beaten the bastard to a pulp.

And enjoyed every blow.

After a long time Erin lay limp in his arms, drained but curiously at peace. She had finally let go. She accepted the handkerchief he gave her, wiping her cheeks.

"I got your shirt all wet," she murmured, her head resting on his shoulder because he still held her tightly.

"It'll dry." Matt rubbed his cheek against her forehead, his voice very gentle.

She realized distantly that Matt could hold her without desire exploding between them, that he could be tender and evoke tenderness, and she pondered that silently. She felt so . . . at home in his arms. Beneath the hand clutching a handkerchief, she could feel his heart beating steadily, his chest rising and falling with each breath.

And she became aware then, very slowly and gently, that she was less confused and uncertain about her own feelings. The dark pain she had hidden away in its locked room had finally burst free, the pain that had been standing between two strangers — and they weren't strangers anymore. There would always be in her a small, empty place nothing would ever fill, but there was no pain now.

One man had hurt her unbearably and another had healed the hurt with a simple touch and gentle sympathy.

Matt was now even more real to her. He was flesh and blood, bone and sinew, and he had shared her pain as instantly and completely as he had shared her anger and her passion. He had not withdrawn from her, had not been awkward or uncertain; his responses to her had been immediate and tender.

Unexpectedly sleepy, Erin tried to hold on to another, more elusive realization. But it slipped away. She fell asleep with the feeling of a heart beating under her hand.

Matt continued to hold her, to softly stroke the silky fire of her hair. He smiled a little, realizing that she'd probably be disgruntled to wake finding herself clinging like a limpet. He was under no illusions; though her painful disclosure had brought them closer than ever before, it had been a temporary closeness. Waking with a clear mind, she would very likely scurry behind her prickly, wary wall, the chip on her shoulder a bit precarious but still visible to the naked eye.

Thorns.

Sometime during the last few moments, Matt had realized wryly that, though their fight had shifted, the battle continued. In passion or pain they could forget differences and share what they felt, but otherwise they circled each other warily.

One year, he thought with a sense of bitterness. One year of her life stood between them. One year and a man who had always been to her something larger than life.

And yet — Matt unknowingly echoed Erin's conclusions — that year had helped to make her the strong woman she was. For good and bad, that year had shaped her. Without a brief, wild ride behind a shining prince, what would she have been today?

Not wary, probably. Not prickly. Not a woman who was finding, now, the depth and power of a woman's feelings. Perhaps without pain she would have remained a princess in search of a prince, or perhaps, as so many had, she would have settled happily for less and built a good life.

Matt rested his chin atop her head and thought about that. He had been, he knew honestly, drawn to her wary independence, her control. An obsession with her face had brought him up here, but it was the personality behind her beauty that had kept him stubbornly in her life. His interest had made him probe, and her challenging response had drawn him even more.

And, of course, there had been his physical reaction to her.

He immediately regretted even the thought. Following the ebbing of pain, desire had crept up on him unawares. The ache that had not entirely deserted him for some time now began throbbing again as he held a sleeping Erin in his arms.

Matt cursed quietly and solemnly. She was half-lying across his lap, and the pressure of her warm body did absolutely nothing to aid him in controlling building desire. In fact, he could almost feel his blood pressure going through the roof, and his body spoke to him emphatically and at some length about stubborn self-denial.

He began reciting verses in a soft and toneless voice, gazing fiercely at a perfectly inoffensive seascape decorating the far wall.

Not that it helped.

Erin thought she was dreaming. A rumbling had disturbed her, finally becoming definite sounds with a kind of rhythm. She listened, frowning a little.

"The Drawling-master was an old conger-eel, that used to come once a week: *he* taught us Drawling, Stretching, and Fainting in Coils."

Definitely, Erin decided, she was dreaming. She frowned harder, eyes tightly closed, and concentrated on the sounds. Surely they'd make sense . . .

But four young oysters hurried up,
  All eager for the treat:
Their coats were brushed, their faces washed,
  Their shoes were clean and neat —
And this was odd, because, you know,
  They hadn't any feet.

Erin sat bolt upright and stared at Matt incredulously. His face, she noted, seemed a bit darker in color than usual, his eyes very bright, and a sheepish smile tugged at his lips.

"Hello." He frowned, cleared his throat, and tried again. This time there was less hoarseness. "You're awake."

"Yes. Are you?"

He tried a careless kind of laugh that broke in the middle — then deepened suddenly in real amusement. "Oh, yes. Yes, I'm awake. Quite painfully awake, in fact."

She frowned at him. "Then why on earth were you reciting Lewis Carroll?"

"It — uh — came most readily to mind. My nephews and nieces all love the verses, so I've memorized most of them."

Erin thought about her question, then clarified it. "Why were you reciting verses of any kind?"

He looked at her for a moment, then sighed. "Because, my darling Erin, it was either recite nonsense verses or else attack you with a howl. A rude awakening for you. I thought the verses would be less likely to earn me a slap."

She blinked. Unaware that she was reacting exactly as Matt had decided she would, she moved abruptly to put nearly a foot of space between them, feeling a bit uneasy over her nap in his arms. And she felt defensive somehow. The combination caused her very understandable reaction.

"Matt, stop pretending you can't keep your hands off me!"

He looked so astonished that she giggled. "Pretending?"

"You're a grown man, for godsake!"

"I keep telling myself that." Matt looked thoughtful and a bit pained. "You probably haven't considered it from my point of view, but I can tell you it's pretty unnerving to find at this late stage in my life that I have so little control over my own body."

Erin lifted a disbelieving eyebrow; she was very conscious of him *and* of her desire, but she felt no urge to howl. An urge to growl, maybe. But not howl. It would be undignified.

In a confiding tone, Matt said, "I probably shouldn't tell you any of this, because you could get drunk with power."

She kept the eyebrow up, but it took an effort.

He crossed his arms over his chest. "I am," he told her courteously, "putty in your hands. You smile at me, and my toes curl. I touch you, and I have to fight the urge to grab you by your hair and drag you off to my cave. When you walk in front of me, I have to concentrate on putting one foot in front of the other. Sleep in my arms, and I have to recite silly verses. I won't even *mention* what happens to me when you're awake and passionate in my embrace."

Erin no longer felt defensive. She felt surprised. Clearing her throat, she murmured, "But you never show it."

"Good. I have some pride." He considered. "Not much, mind you, but some."

She hesitated, then said almost inaudibly, "We can still take the easy way."

He reached over to brush his knuckles down her cheek briefly. The eyes that had half-laughed at her before darkened now, and his voice was a little husky. "No. When you can wake up in my arms and not pull away — then it'll be time for the easy way. And the easy way will be the right way."

Her throat felt tight in the most ridiculous way, and she fought to ignore it. Inexplicably cross, she muttered, "I'm not likely to wake up in your arms again unless we *do* take the easy way!"

His eyes were laughing again. "There is that. I'll have to arrange something."

Erin felt slightly baffled and extremely wary. Though more certain now of her own feelings, she was still unsure of his. He wanted her — she didn't doubt that. He *said* he wanted her love; he made use of occasional endearments; he had certainly shown her tenderness and understanding. Yet she was still uneasy. He had not offered his own love, although she thought he had nearly done so after telling her she'd have to face Stuart before they could go on.

She remembered his challenge then. He

hadn't offered his love — but he had invited her to take it. His heart.

"You're thinking again," he noted dryly.

Slowly, Erin rose to her feet and stretched like a cat. She didn't think about what she was doing until Matt muttered something, and she looked at him in surprise that became quick comprehension. "Sorry," she murmured, pulling her sweater hastily back down over her midriff.

He was looking at her with a curiously twisted smile. "I," he said, "am certifiably out of my mind." He laughed.

She stood with her hands on her hips and stared at him, still frowning just a bit, her mind working. "Yes," she said finally. "Yes, I think you are."

"Meaning?"

"Why look so surprised?" she inquired mildly. "I was just agreeing with you."

"Yes," he said, studying her oddly immobile expression. "But what did you mean by it?"

"I mean . . . you're crazy because you've put both of us on an emotional roller coaster. Neither of us — apparently — can think straight when we — when we touch each other." She took a deep breath, then rushed on. "Nothing matters then, nothing seems impossible. But then we aren't touching, and — and it doesn't seem real."

He rose to his feet, frowning. "Erin —"

"You seem real," she hurried on. "And when I look at you, I know — I know there's . . . something between us. Something real. It's *me*, Matt. It's what I feel that I don't trust, don't believe in."

"Give it time," he urged quietly.

"I . . . don't think we have much time." *Before we lose control,* she added silently. *Before we take a step that can never be taken back, a step that will change us forever.* She brushed a hand through her hair, frowning. "Matt . . . I have to think this time. I *have* to. I won't be swept away again. And I think — I think I can write now. I think I need to."

"Are you telling me to get lost?" His voice was still quiet, but a little strained now.

Erin turned away, going to the door and gazing out blindly. "I'm . . . asking. How long will Stuart be in Denver? Do you know?"

"He's giving three concerts, the last one a week from tonight. Apparently, the demand for his concerts took three scheduled performances to satisfy."

She nodded. "It has before." After a moment she said, "Then give me a week, Matt. A week to be alone, to write. To think."

"Are you afraid of facing him?"

"No." She turned then, leaning back against the doorjamb. "No, I'm not afraid. Instead of tomorrow night, we — I'll — face him in a week."

"We," Matt said flatly. "We'll face him. If you want me to leave, Erin, then I will. But I'll be with you in Denver next week, at that concert." He was silent for a moment, then added ruefully, "Well, I came up here to find out why you weren't writing and to try to help. Try to shake something loose. It looks like I've done that, at least."

"At least." She smiled a little. "I guess after three years of peace and quiet I needed a jolt. You were right about that, I think."

He studied her, his eyes restless, then sighed. "I'll call Steve and have him come pick me up. But I'll be back, Erin. Next Friday."

She stared after him for a long moment, hearing his deep voice in the radio room. Then she went out and sat on the steps, asking herself if she was doing the right thing. She thought she was. It was true — she needed time. She had been carried along in a breathless rush after meeting Stuart; she didn't want to wake one day and find that the explosion of feeling between her and Matt had carried her blindly a second time.

She felt his presence even before he sat down beside her, and spoke without thinking. "I should have met you first."

"But you didn't." There was a faint smile in his voice. "You met him. And you were looking for a prince."

"Was I? If so, it was stupid of me. Fairy tales. I reached for glitter . . . and that's what I got. Just something shiny and empty." Staring blindly she said, "There's nothing *there* anymore, Matt. Just a year gone from my life. Why can't I forget it? Why can't I put it behind me?"

"Because vows mean something to you." He didn't touch her, and his voice was low, taut. "Because you married a man and lost a dream . . . and a child." After a moment, and with obvious reluctance, he went on quietly. "There is something there, Erin. Something you haven't resolved. Him. To you, he was always larger than life. He wrecked your dreams, but he never quite forced you to let go of them. Not all of them. There's still something in you that blames yourself instead of him. That's what you can't let go of."

Against her will, listening to his low, relentless voice, Erin realized he was right. There *was* a part of her that was afraid she had been somehow inadequate, a part of her that had numbly accepted a large part of the blame.

"It takes two," she whispered. "Two to make a marriage. Two to destroy it." She had thought it before. Seen it before. But she hadn't realized, hadn't understood.

They both heard the sound of a helicopter approaching, and Matt rose to his feet. Catching her hands, he pulled her up as well. Quickly, he said, "Sometimes it only takes one. Erin . . . he'll try to get you back."

She looked up at him, bewildered. "No. Not Stuart."

"Yes." Matt was speaking a little louder now as the thumping sound of rotors grew closer. "He's shallow and he's a fool, but he'll see the change in you. It'll gall him, Erin. He'll hate the fact that another man found something in you that he missed, something he never touched." Matt glanced up, impatient, as the roar of Steve's helicopter grew louder.

"Matt, you're wrong! He doesn't care —"

Running out of time, Matt bent his head to kiss her hard. "Just listen to me," he said. "I know what I'm saying, Erin! And I want you to think about that. God knows I don't want to do anything to send you back to him — but you have to know. You could handle him now. You could have him on his *knees!*

You're a hell of a lot stronger than he is. Remember that."

Then, after another hard, possessive kiss, Matt was gone.

Making use of the earphones he and his passenger wore, Steve said cheerfully, "Now *that* was a leave-taking! When're you going to introduce me to that gorgeous redhead?"

Matt managed to find a calm voice in the tumult of his emotions. "Pull your tongue back in. Ally wouldn't like it."

Virtuously, Steve retorted, "Ally knows I'd never stray. That doesn't mean I'm dead, however. Do I hear wedding bells, Matt?"

A bit grimly, Matt answered, "I certainly hope so. You wouldn't happen to have a lance lying around handy, would you?"

With a sidelong glance from merry brown eyes, Steve said gravely, "I put mine away in mothballs after I won Ally. Why? Don't tell me you've been challenged?"

"I think I'm about to be. An ex-husband, damn his soul." Matt wondered a bit desperately if he'd done the right thing in warning Erin. He just didn't know. But he was certain that Stuart Travis would try his damnedest to recapture his ex-wife, and he didn't want Erin swept blindly off her feet again.

At least she'd *know* this time.

If only, he thought, she could come to terms with her marriage before she met Travis again. Heaven knew she had the strength, now, to resist the man's apparent charm — except that she didn't realize that. Matt knew he could spark her anger, and in anger she would fight fiercely for control. But Travis had been unable to spark those strong feelings while they were married.

Could he sweep her off her feet a second time? Was there enough guilt within Erin to force her to make a last effort to live up to those vows she believed in?

Or would these new, stronger feelings give her the strength to finally let go of her image of her ex-husband?

"You look dangerous," Steve commented lightly but with an undertone of concern.

Matt watched as the little town at the base of the mountains grew nearer. "I feel it," he confessed. "My entire future depends on what happens next Friday. And I have an awful feeling that a lance won't help me. Dammit, I should have taken the easy way."

Steve glanced at his longtime friend and said dryly, "I won't ask you to define that." He cleared his throat. "Will you be going back up there tomorrow?"

"No. No, she doesn't want that. I'll be

going back to New York for a few days." As the helicopter set down near his motel, Matt turned in his seat to gaze at Steve. "But there *is* something you can do for me."

"Name it."

Erin moved by rote, taking care of her horses and making peace with a sulky Chester. She didn't want to think about what Matt had said to her, and managed to blank her mind until she was in bed that night. But then . . .

Would Stuart want her now? Would he, as Matt had so flatly stated, try to get her back?

And how did she feel about that?

Erin could admit to herself now that she felt guilty, inadequate about the past. Her marriage had failed. She had failed. No matter how many times she had told herself that Stuart had stripped her bare and stood her before the world, a small part of her wondered if she should have been able to cope with that, change it.

"You could handle him now. You could have him on his knees! You're a hell of a lot stronger than he is — remember that."

Being human, Erin thought for a fleeting moment of bringing Stuart to his knees, and how it would feel. Then she realized that it would feel empty. She didn't want Stuart —

not even at her feet.

Her guilt and uncertainty were still with her, though. Was she so afraid that a second relationship would find her inadequate, so afraid of failing again? Was that why she was, even now, wary of her feelings for Matt?

There was much she still didn't know about him. He was not, as Stuart had been, an image of something more than a man. But he was, in his own way, elusive, not quite real. He had startling good looks, charm, humor, intelligence, and compassion.

He was a flesh-and-blood reality — and yet she knew little about him, and that made him elusive. He was so adaptable that she had no idea what his preferences were. He had come out of nowhere to enter her life and jar her from the peaceful limbo she had built for herself, yet he had revealed very little of himself in the process.

Or . . . had he? What did she really know, with certainty, about Matt Gavin? As to background, she knew only where he'd grown up and gone to school, that he had four sisters. As to the man that background had produced, she knew that he understood women uncannily well. That he felt a deep respect for writers and was a staunch supporter of creative freedom.

She knew that he was sensitive, under-standing, compassionate. That he could make her laugh and rage and cry in spite of herself. That he could evoke passions more powerful than she would have believed possible.

In astonishment, Erin realized that she knew an awful lot about Matt, especially considering the short time since they had met.

Why, then, did he seem so elusive?

Because you aren't looking at him. Stuart's glitter blinded you, and you're so afraid it'll happen again that you won't look at Matt. He isn't elusive. You just don't trust yourself to reach out and touch him.

Erin drew a deep, slow breath and stared at a dark ceiling. Was that it, then? She had to look at Stuart without his glitter, and she had to look at Matt without the fear of being blinded.

Princes. All the thoughts, comparisons, analogies. She had always thought of Stuart as a prince, and when Matt had appeared, she had quickly, instinctively, thought of him that way as well.

Why?

Simple. So simple now that she faced it. Princes were dreams — vague, untouchable things conjured from wisps of imagination.

Not real. They blinded one with the glitter of their perfection.

There was, in a prince, no need for reality. And relationships with princes conjured emotions just as unreal. In love — with the idea of being in love.

Safe. Nothing real to touch.

But Matt, whether consciously or not, had refused to be safe. Needling, probing, purposely pricking his fingers on the thorns she surrounded herself with. He was a flesh-and-blood man who demanded equal reality from a woman. A man who demanded the *real* passions instead of girlish wistfulness.

And that was what Erin was wary of, mistrustful of.

She had failed to cope with a dream. And she was afraid she would fail even more devastatingly to cope with reality.

In Matt's arms, with the explosion of desire between them, she touched reality — and gloried in it.

But then, inevitably, she backed away, unnerved. Tried to convince herself that it was the *desire* and her own feelings that were unreal. Because dreams were safe.

She fumbled toward understanding, even as sleep finally claimed her.

Chapter Seven

In the three years since she had lived on the mountain, Erin had never felt loneliness. After the frenetic pace of her marriage, she had been more than ready for aloneness. But now, as the days passed, she felt lonely.

There was an emptiness she'd never known before, a place where something *should* have been . . . and wasn't.

She leaned heavily on her writing during those days, working long hours and skipping both meals and sleep. She felt a rueful gratitude that Matt, in throwing her emotions into chaos, had somehow forced her to break through her "story block" and begin writing again. Her book began taking shape, paragraph following paragraph on her computer's screen, her thoughts fixed firmly on the story.

But when the computer was shut off and the silence of night closed in around her, Erin found herself restless and anxious. She had talked to Mal on the radio on Saturday and his news of Matt's leaving had depressed her. She didn't — oddly enough —

doubt that he would return; it was just that he was so far away.

She dreamed about him, unsettling dreams she could never remember clearly. She thought about him almost constantly, wondering what she would see when she finally *did* look at him, finally did reach out to him.

It didn't occur to her until Tuesday night that she had not thought of Stuart, had not compared him and Matt in days. And she realized that she hadn't because Matt was so strongly in the foreground of her thoughts, so solidly real; there was no longer room even for the glitter that was Stuart. The realization made her feel stronger, more positive about her relationship with Matt.

She was dividing men from princes.

Erin honestly didn't know if Stuart would remain wrapped in the armor she had seen so clearly. She didn't know if he would, now, become just a man in her eyes. She thought somehow that he would not, that Stuart Travis *was* something larger than life. That he was, in fact, untouchable.

The thought brought her no grief, no interest. Whatever Stuart was, she no longer wanted.

She *would* face Stuart and put him and her guilt behind her. And then, with luck, she could build something with Matt.

On Wednesday morning Erin woke to a thumping roar, and she recognized the sound of *Bolero* and the arrival of a helicopter. She threw back the covers and hurried to the front door, her heart thudding, hoping that Matt had returned in spite of her week limit. But when she yanked open the door, it was to see the helicopter lifting off and swooping away.

Bewildered, she gazed after it until she could neither see it nor hear the fanfare of music. Disappointment tightened her throat and she swore unsteadily. It was then, backing away a step and beginning to close the door, that Erin looked down to see the roses.

Six perfect red roses wrapped in tissue, and atop them lay an envelope.

Erin carried the roses into the cabin and lay them on the bar, feeling unexpectedly teary. She opened the envelope carefully, and unfolded a short message.

I never minded thorns, but six days without you are hard to bear. I hope you're missing me. A favor? I've asked Steve to come and pick you up early Thursday morning; please stay with him and his wife in Denver until I arrive.

They want to meet you, and have invited you to stay as long as you like. Bring Chester; Jake tells me you can pasture the horses. Please, Erin, do this for me.

There was never a week so long.

Matt

Erin had to laugh a few minutes later when she found herself standing before her closet debating what to take with her to Denver. There was, she realized, just something about Matt Gavin. He was like an elemental force driving all before it. He asked her to go and stay with total strangers and await his arrival — and she was going to do just that.

After packing with a cheerfulness she couldn't remember ever feeling before, Erin completed the other chores necessary for leaving. Perishable foodstuffs were carried some distance from the cabin and left for foraging animals. Riding Amos and leading Tucker, she took the horses farther up the mountain to a large canyon, where there was plentiful pasture, a sparkling stream, and shelter from harsh weather.

With Chester for company, she made her way leisurely back to the cabin, asking herself if she could leave all this. The answer, honestly, was no. Not forever. But she had gradually come to realize that she no longer felt any fear or discomfort at the thought of living in a city; that fear had simply been caused by memories of too many hours alone during her marriage. It was not the *place*, she realized now, that mattered.

This mountain had helped to heal her, and it would always be a place to come back to. But she thought that — perhaps — she could stand time away. Even months. As long as there was this to return to.

Not to run to. Erin didn't plan on running again.

She was ready early the next morning, bag packed and by the door. The generator was off, the cabin silent. Chester was grumbling uneasily and tried to hide from her as she found his leash, recognizing, as animals often do, the indications of departure.

Erin cornered him and fastened the leash, laughing. "No, Chester — not the vet, I promise. We're going visiting."

Chester howled when Ravel approached, but stopped suddenly as the music and engine did. Holding the leash firmly since her pet was not above making a dash for freedom, Erin opened the door to look curiously at the approaching pilot.

He was a lean six-footer, dark-haired,

with cheerful brown eyes, dressed as casually as she in jeans and a sweat shirt. His voice was deep and lilting when he spoke.

"Steve Burke," he said, holding out a lean hand.

Erin shook hands, smiling because people would always smile at so cheerful a man. "Erin Scott. It's nice to finally meet you after hearing you come and go so many times."

He grinned. "Have to do justice to Sadie, you know. Besides — I like to see people react." He glanced at her bag, his lean face relaxing somewhat. "Good — then you are coming."

"Did you doubt it?" she asked curiously.

"Well, Matt didn't," he said, then immediately grimaced. "I didn't mean that the way it sounded."

She was laughing. "Yes, I know. He wasn't arrogant about it. He just knew I'd come. Damn him."

Clearly reassured by this reaction, Steve smiled again. "Ally's really looking forward to it. My wife — Alison." He looked past her to Chester's crouched, rebellious form and said cheerfully, "Hello, Chester. Ready for a ride?"

Chester lifted a lip at him.

Laughing, Steve carried Erin's bag to the

helicopter, then returned to help her muscle the reluctant dog into his place behind the seats. Within moments Sadie lifted away, the sounds of Chester's unhappiness drowned by rotors.

Making use of the earphones, Steve explained that he and his wife had a house in the suburbs of Denver. He replied to Erin's hesitant question that they had two children — Danny and Julie, eight and six respectively.

He cheerfully dismissed Erin's fears that having her stay with them would be an imposition, then talked to her easily during the ride to Denver.

"How long have you known Matt?" she asked at one point.

"Twenty years. We met in high school. Went to the same college. Same branch of the service, too."

"Service?"

"Air Force. We were both pilots." He sent her a sudden grin. "They were glad to get rid of me, but tried everything short of blackmail to keep Matt; he's a natural pilot. We both learned as teenagers, because Matt's mother is a pilot."

Erin listened, fascinated. "Is she? He didn't mention it."

Steve laughed. "I'm not surprised. There

isn't a lot he could say about her with a straight face. His mother — like yours truly — is a seat-of-the-pants pilot. I'm being careful today," he added cheerfully, "since Matt told me he'd draw and quarter me otherwise."

She blinked, then laughed. "I see. Go on about his mother."

"Her name's Penelope, absurd as it sounds. But Penny to everyone who knows her — including air traffic controllers who have conspired with Matt from time to time to keep her grounded. Matt even hid her plane a few years ago. Not that it did any good."

"What happened?"

"She bought another one."

"Good heavens." Erin hesitated, then asked carefully, "Is she so dangerous a pilot?"

"Oh, no, not dangerous. Just . . . gleeful. Apt to do chancy things. Matt only just stopped her once from joining a stunt team."

Erin felt her eyes widening, and a giggle caught in her throat. The "traditional" East indeed! she thought. No wonder Matt had looked peculiar when she'd made that remark. And no wonder he'd developed the gift of laughter; he'd had a choice of laughter or despair with such a mother!

"Does she still — ?"

"Oh, yes. Penny's forever young. She's in her late fifties, of course, but she married young. The twins were born when she was just nineteen."

"Twins?"

"He didn't tell you? Well, Matt doesn't talk about family much. His oldest sisters are twins, Adrian and Barbara. After them came Kathy, then Matt, then Ally." Abruptly, Steve winced and sent her an uneasy look.

Erin hadn't missed it. "Ally. Alison? Your wife?"

He sighed. "Well, she would have told you once we got home. It's just that Matt said you wouldn't come if you knew."

"He was right." Erin had to laugh, though. "So he's your brother-in-law."

"And best friend," Steve said with the deceptively casual sound of bedrock certainty. Then in a suddenly teasing voice he added, "Of course, he never listens to my advice. I warned him, for instance, that a Scots-Irish girl was more than most men could handle. *Especially* a redhead. But he's mostly Welsh himself, and those Celts always do like a challenge."

Erin managed to speak lightly. "You

speak from experience?"

"About Celts, I sure do. *All* the Gavins enjoy challenge. About redheaded Scots-Irish girls . . . well, let's just say I know what dynamite looks like."

Erin would have responded to that — although she wasn't sure just how — but the helicopter began descending then, and she took the time to gather her composure. It had been no part of her plans to meet any of Matt's family, particularly now, when she was still uncertain.

However . . .

In the sprawling two-story house that was comfortably cluttered, evidence of an active family, Alison Burke greeted Erin with cheerful friendliness. She was nearly as tall as Erin, dark-haired and blue-eyed, and looked ten years younger than she was.

"Nice meeting you, Erin. Is this — well, of course it is. Matt described him, but — Hello, Chester. He can have the run of the house, Erin, and our backyard's fenced."

They had left the helicopter a mile down the road at a private airstrip, and Erin's dog had only just stopped grumbling about his unexpected ride. Steve took her bag upstairs, disappearing just as two dark-haired urchins erupted from another room to fall on Chester with uninhibited cries.

Erin, secure in the knowledge that Chester was a marshmallow with children, watched with a smile as Ally tried to talk above the noise.

"Danny and Julie," she told Erin wryly. "And they love animals so much they're inclined to forget manners. Get up, you monsters, and say hello to Erin!"

Two pairs of identical blue eyes gleamed up at her, and childish voices found politeness for a moment. "Hello, Erin," they said in unison, then instantly fell to arguing over who was to have the honor of shaking the paw Chester amiably waved at them.

Ally drew Erin into the family room and smiled. "I'm glad they're fussing over him; our ten-year-old collie died last year, and they've refused another dog. I think it's time now." Her blue eyes were bright as she studied Erin with friendly curiosity.

Seeing hesitation, Erin put the older woman at ease. "Steve let the cat out of the bag," she said dryly. "And I just may kill your brother when he gets here."

Ally laughed and waved her guest to a chair. "He does have an uncomfortable way of understanding what you'd rather he didn't," she agreed. "But in this case, I'm glad. Any woman who can get my brother on a horse is one I want to meet!"

Hearing something in Ally's voice, Erin looked at her curiously. "He just wanted to find a reclusive writer," she explained, "and horseback was the only way."

"Yes," Ally agreed, smiling. "But it's funny, don't you think? Odd, I mean. He stayed here for a few days before he set out to look for you. He mentioned that one of his writers lived up on some mountain near here. But he didn't say anything about going to find you. Steve and I've read your books, by the way, and enjoyed them immensely."

"Thank you," Erin said rather blankly, wondering at the gleeful look in Ally's eyes.

With elaborate casualness Ally said, "He soaks up information like a sponge, you know. Matt. Always interested in whatever's happening. We're all pack rats in a way, saving newspapers and magazines. And Matt's always looking for ideas, of course, to suggest to some of his writers. So he goes through my stuff whenever he's here."

From the doorway, Steve said ruefully, "Matt's going to kill you, Ally."

She laughed and agreed, "Probably!"

"What's going on?" Erin asked, baffled. She looked from husband to wife, seeing a laughing despair on Steve's face and gleeful enjoyment on Ally's. "Somebody clue me in?"

Ally looked back at their guest as Steve came to sit beside her on the couch. "Gladly. You see, Matt found something unexpected among my newspapers and magazines."

"What?"

"His Waterloo." Ally giggled suddenly. "I came in here and found him surrounded by dusty newspapers — the Denver papers — and he looked like the house had fallen in on him. Sort of stunned and incredulous."

"What was it?" Erin was completely at sea.

"It was," Ally told her enjoyably, "a picture and part of an article. Only part, unfortunately; probably the kids had torn away the rest."

Apparently deciding that his wife wouldn't listen to the voice of reason, Steve chimed in ruefully with the rest. "The picture was one an enterprising reporter had snapped in a town not far from here. A picture of a reclusive writer. He used a telephoto lens, by the way. Apparently, he'd had some experience of the writer's wrath earlier, and was still smarting under a load of buckshot. Can't blame him, I suppose, for standing well back when he took the picture."

"That'll teach me to make an enemy of reporters," Erin agreed dryly. She took a good look at their faces, and her own went still. "Matt would have recognized the pen name, of course," she said slowly.

Seriously, Ally said, "He cares very much about writers, you know. And he was worried about you because he believed you were having trouble with your work." Then, in a very deliberate tone, she added, "But he hardly got on a horse — after avoiding them religiously for thirty-five years — and climbed a mountain just to find a reclusive writer. He went to find the woman in that picture."

Perhaps it shouldn't have been a shock. Erin had wondered, after all, at Matt's apparently sudden interest. She thought back to that first meeting and shook her head disbelievingly. "He didn't know me. He asked about —"

"Devious, my brother. And when he wants, he's got the best poker face this side of a riverboat gambler. Erin, Matt went up there to find *you*, not a writer. He carries that picture in his wallet."

Erin had to think about that. And both Ally and Steve, realizing, immediately dropped the subject.

The rest of the day was enjoyable for Erin.

The Burke family accepted her casually. Erin found herself asking about the entire Gavin family and being answered easily, and she learned all about the fascinating Penny, about Matt's sisters and their families. And about Matt.

Moment by moment he grew more real to her. And with Ally's astounding information in the back of her mind, she found herself inwardly going back over her time with Matt.

She found it difficult to believe that he had, as Ally had heavily implied, fallen in love with a picture. Yet she couldn't help but remember his determination to remain with her, to get to know her.

To box shadows.

He called late that afternoon, talking briefly to his sister before asking for Erin. And Erin, who could also play poker, held her hand very close to her chest.

"Hello, Matt," she said calmly, glancing around at the den, which had been tactfully vacated by Steve and Ally.

"I miss you," he told her, his voice husky.

Erin ignored her weakening knees and kept her voice calm. "Do you? I got some writing done this week."

"Good." But he sounded restless. "You

aren't mad at me, are you? For not telling you who Ally and Steve were?"

"Do I sound mad?"

"You sound like a prickly rose bush," he answered wryly.

"You said you didn't mind thorns." She spoke without thinking.

"No. No, I don't mind *your* thorns." He paused. "I'll be back tomorrow afternoon, Erin. And I've gotten our seats for the concert." It was a question.

Steadily, Erin answered it. "All right."

"And then we go on." He sounded restless again. "Erin . . . remember what I told you, will you? You're stronger now. Stronger than he is."

"All right," she repeated, unemotional.

Matt swore softly. "I'll see you tomorrow, then."

"Yes. Good-bye, Matt."

She stood for a moment, staring down at the telephone. Then, taking a deep breath, she picked up the receiver again and made a collect call. In California, the call was accepted, with surprise, and Erin kept her own voice even and mildly friendly.

"Hello, Con, how are you?"

"Fine, just fine, Erin. And you?" Conrad Styles, Stuart's manager, hid his surprise swiftly with the expertise of years.

She more or less passed over his question. "Con, I'm in Denver, and I'd like to see Stuart. Can you tell me where he's staying, please?" Experience told her that Stuart's whereabouts would be a closely guarded secret, as always, to prevent hordes of fans from descending on the hotel.

After a slight hesitation Con said slowly, "Stuart told me that if you ever got in touch, I was to let him know pronto. Seems your lawyer's a bit protective and won't give out your address."

Erin was a little surprised, and slightly wary. "Did Stuart want to get in touch with me for any special reason?"

"He didn't say. I told him he could write through your lawyer, but he wasn't having any. It must have been a few months ago, I guess." He hesitated, then said unemotionally. "Lisa didn't last out the divorce proceedings. Did you know?"

"No." But Erin wasn't surprised. Lisa, the "other woman" Stuart had written about. Dryly, she added, "No reconciliation, Con. I just want to talk to Stuart. Will you tell me where he's staying?"

Quietly, Con gave her the hotel and room number. Then, slowly and to Erin's surprise, he added, "Stuart's a fantastic talent, Erin, but he'll always be a taker. Don't let him take anything else from you, huh? I didn't like what he did to you before."

Erin was touched, remembering only then that it had been Con who had sometimes made things bearable by seeing to it that she was rarely trapped in hotel rooms while Stuart practiced and performed; he had often cheerfully played tourist with her just so she could see various cities.

"Thanks for caring, Con. But I've made a new life for myself — and there's someone else now. Stuart won't hurt me again."

"I hope not," Con said soberly. "Take care, Erin."

"I will. Good-bye, Con."

Erin debated briefly, but she knew that her mind had been made up even before her call to Stuart's manager. She had to see him alone, without Matt to cling to. Matt, she thought ruefully, would not be happy about it. But he would, she knew, understand.

Casually, Erin told her hosts that she was going into Denver for a while that night, and was instantly urged to take one of the family cars. Gratefully accepting, she left soon after dinner, armed with a map and feeling curiously calm and detached.

She had dressed with no special care, wearing dark slacks and a coral silk blouse.

Light makeup, as usual. She wore her hair in a single braid hanging down her back.

She had no trouble finding the small hotel, and went inside with the casual air of belonging. She went directly to the elevators, up to Stuart's floor, and found herself knocking on his door — only then wondering with amusement if she would be interrupting the current romance.

She did not.

Stuart opened the door swiftly, saying impatiently, "It's about time —" Then broke off to stare at her in surprise. "Erin!"

"Hello, Stuart. Mind if I come in?" Her voice was calm, casual.

"Of course not." He stepped back, gesturing, and Erin entered his room. Suite, really; it was brightly lit, because Stuart couldn't bear dim rooms, and empty of people but for them.

Erin crossed to the center of the sitting room before turning to face him, feeling a faint, thoughtful surprise. How odd, she mused; he was only as tall as she was herself. She could have sworn he was taller.

Maybe it was true, then, that the people and places in one's past were always smaller than they were remembered to be.

"I was expecting room service," Stuart said more or less automatically, doing a bit of stocktaking himself. Vivid blue eyes looked her over thoroughly, a speculative gleam hovering somewhere in their depths.

He has an idea, she realized with more resignation than annoyance.

"What're you doing in Denver?" Stuart asked.

"Visiting friends."

"Does that include me?"

"No." She smiled a little. "We were never friends."

"We were lovers," he said with surprising truculence. "We were married."

Erin studied him in silence, trying to remember back to the days when that fierceness in his voice had shaken her, made her anxious. At that moment she could remember the emotions analytically — but felt nothing except faint interest.

How volatile he was, she thought. Like a child — or a superstar. He was constantly needing, his hot emotions quickly past and forgotten. Consciously or unconsciously, he was certain that the entire universe revolved around him.

He was lean with the wired tautness of explosive energy. Dark and brooding of face. Undeniably, strikingly handsome. Women had been known to do incredible things to get his attention.

But . . . A little surprised, Erin saw a man instead of a prince, and wondered how she could have been so blind.

She went to a chair and sat down, feeling unthreatened and unafraid. "Con said you wanted to see me. Any particular reason?"

His brows drew together as he stood staring at her. Indecision and uncertainty flickered in his eyes, then anger. The anger of a man accustomed to holding the complete attention of whomever he spoke to. "I want you back," he said roughly.

It was, Erin thought vaguely, a suitably dramatic line delivered with suitable fire. Ruined, though, by the knock at the door announcing room service.

She was so delighted to find that his words left her unmoved that she was smiling when the door closed behind the waiter and Stuart faced her again.

"Erin —" He stepped toward her, eyes lighting.

"No." She shook her head, stopping him in midstride. "I'm sorry, Stuart. There's nothing between us now. Surely you can see that?"

"I want you back," he said stubbornly, fiercely.

She shook her head again. "I have a new life now, one I'm quite happy with." She thought of Matt, and her lips curved unconsciously.

Stuart went very still, something hot and angry leaping out of his eyes. "And another man?"

Erin looked at him. "Did you think," she said dryly, "I'd waste away for wanting you? If you'll cast your mind back, you'll remember that I left you. And that's where it ended, Stuart."

"I'll change your mind," he promised, arrogant and certain.

It took only a moment for Erin to realize what he was doing. She found herself wondering ruefully how she had truly believed him in the past. Stuart was surely playing a role. He was fathoms deep in the role of a lover betrayed, a lover desperate to reclaim his lost love no matter what the cost to his pride.

He probably believed it himself, she thought, after so many years of the same sort of ordeal. And it was an ordeal for him, she knew. He would tear himself to shreds — for a while. Then he would set the emotions to music, and blast them into an audience of millions of adoring fans.

And the emotions would be forgotten, with no lingering pain.

It was sad. For the first time, she understood what his genius cost him. His own demon drove him to experience — however briefly — all the extremes of emotion; and his life was a series of roles designed spontaneously for just that effect.

He had, she realized then, played the part of a shining prince with the same deliberate spontaneity. He had found a princess and had supplied a prince, automatically and with pleasure, as any actor would throw himself delightedly into a new and challenging role. And then the part of husband and — briefly — expectant father. Then erring husband, ashamed and suffering. Ending, finally, with the noble pain of a husband releasing his wife.

And now he was arrogant and demanding, but pleading underneath, striving to win back the ex-wife that his own careless cruelty had driven away from him.

Erin felt no desire to laugh. And, perhaps oddly, no desire to lash out at him for the pain he had caused. One could hardly, she thought, punish a demon.

Instead, she found herself rising with a grave face. Found herself — for the first time — knowingly and willingly supplying fodder for his song. She looked at him with eyes holding just a touch of sad regret — and it was not acting on her part. She was sad for him, and regretful that he would never know the true magic of feelings that he allowed himself to feel only for a while.

"I'm sorry, Stuart." She found, instinctively, lines to add to his play. "Once we might have tried again. But it's too late now. And you . . . you belong to the world. There was never a part of you that was mine. I need a man who can give himself to me. A man who needs me."

"I need you!" His face was drawn, pale.

"You need your music." She moved toward the door slowly.

Stuart reached out suddenly, blind obsession in his eyes. He caught her before she could escape, pinning her wrists at the small of her back and kissing her with bruising passion.

Erin stood unmoved, not struggling, no flicker of response rising in her. She could have told him that it was never his passion that had attracted or held her, never physical desire she had responded to. That he had made her breathless, but had never touched her with fire.

But that would have ruined his play.

When he finally lifted his head and gazed with clouded eyes into her own distant face, Stuart's mouth twisted bitterly. "I killed it, didn't I?" he asked huskily. "I killed it three years ago."

Erin looked at him mutely.

With a curse Stuart released her. He turned toward the room's small bar and fumbled to make himself a drink. Abruptly, he turned back, staring at her. And there might have been a flicker of honest regret in his eyes.

"You woke up. Grew up. Because of another man."

Her instant surprise quickly faded. Of course he saw a change in her — just as Matt had predicted. And he was, underneath the layers of genius, man enough to understand.

"We'll be at your concert tomorrow night," she said slowly, unsure why she was telling him.

"He wants a look at his competition?" Stuart laughed harshly before she could respond. "I always thought you had fire buried somewhere. And, damn you, I could never find it."

She blinked, again surprised, but Stuart was instantly back in his role.

"I won't give up, Erin. I'll win you back."

Erin gathered her thoughts and played her part. "No, Stuart. It's too late. I won't be seeing you again after tomorrow. There wouldn't be any use."

He watched, grim and unsmiling, as she headed for the door. When she turned for a last look, his eyes were bright . . . and she could almost hear the music. She went from the room, closing the door behind her quietly.

She stood silently in the hall for long moments, until she heard what she had expected to hear. The sounds of tentative chords being struck on a guitar.

He had given her a glorious, painful ride on a white charger. He had given her a crown of sorts. He had blinded her with shining armor and left her breathless. He had rocked her off the stable foundations of her life and forced her to stand alone. He had stripped her naked before the world.

And now he was just a memory, the ragged, painful edges of it smoothed by understanding and pity. Now he was just a man who sang songs born in fleeting emotions. A man who would never know he had missed the best song of all.

Erin touched the door briefly with her fingers and turned away from the sounds of birth.

Now he was just a man.

And she wondered . . .

What price genius . . . ?

When Erin left the hotel, she drove aimlessly for a while. Thinking. Remembering pain that was distant now and unimportant. Thinking of the deep and honest emotions Matt had sparked in her.

No wonder, she thought, Stuart had never managed to touch the deepest part of her. His talent had made him a manipulator, a taker; he delved within himself for the frantic surge of momentary emotion and played off those nearby for the responses he needed. And anyone near, dazed by his charisma, inevitably played the roles assigned to them.

But those others lost something of themselves, and Stuart never did. He was, as always, a man driven, obsessed.

She wondered again if he would ever know the real thing. Ever allow himself to feel honest emotion that would never find its way into a song. Perhaps. But Erin didn't think so, and she was glad that Stuart himself would in all probability never realize he had missed something so special.

Erin drove back to the suburbs and parked in the Burkes' driveway. It was late, but they had left the front porch light on for her and given her a key. She let herself in quietly, closed and locked the door, and turned off the porch light.

A small lamp stood on the hall table by the stairs, providing a warm, dim glow. And when he spoke, she turned toward the den to find his face in shadow, his body taut.

"You went to see him."

Chapter Eight

"I went to see him." She moved slowly toward the den, past Matt when he stepped back. The room was lighted only by a lamp next to the couch. An ashtray on the coffee table was overflowing. Clearly, Matt had waited restlessly a long time for her to come back.

She sat down on the couch, laying her purse absently aside, only then meeting his eyes as he sat down a foot or so away.

He looked strained, and his face was almost imperceptibly thinner, the fine bones more prominent. The gray eyes were intent, worried.

Without hesitation, she smiled at him.

Matt relaxed somewhat, eyes instantly brighter, smiling in response. He half-turned toward her, but didn't touch her or move closer. "You had to see him alone," he said.

Erin nodded, hearing both his understanding of that and his dislike of it. "It was important, Matt. It had to be just him and me, with no audience. No one to . . . act for."

"And?" He looked at her, eyes restless.

Erin didn't hesitate. She told him exactly what had happened, sparing neither Matt nor herself. She told him all the things she had realized and understood. And she finished by telling him of the song being written even now.

After her voice had trailed away, Matt said reluctantly, "I can almost feel sorry for him."

"I do." She smiled a little. "But that's all I feel. I don't love him or hate him or feel bitter toward him."

Huskily, Matt said, "Then that year isn't standing between us anymore?"

"No."

"But . . . you still have to hear him sing. It was his singing, wasn't it, that first drew you?"

Erin no longer felt surprise at Matt's perception. She nodded. "He's larger than life onstage. It was easy to look at him and see a prince. But it won't make a difference now, Matt."

"Still." He sighed. "Until you're absolutely sure . . ."

"I can't sleep in your arms?" There was a faint note of teasing in her voice but a stronger note of longing.

"I don't think," he said, clearing his

throat, "that I could stand it."

"You said you missed me," she murmured.

Matt looked at her for a moment, then said rather grimly, "You know what hurts almost more than anything? My jaw. My teeth have been gritted ever since I left you."

She reached out to touch his lean face, her fingers gentle. "I'm sorry."

He half-closed his eyes at her touch, and a muscle leaped under her fingers. "You've been driving me crazy," he said in a strained but conversational tone. "Ever since the day we met."

Erin hid an inward smile and said gravely, "Steve said he warned you. About redheaded Scots-Irish girls. You should have listened to him."

"Next time," Matt said a bit thickly, "I will."

"And I," she said, "will be nicer to journalists next time. Then they won't hide behind things and take pictures."

Matt's eyes, dark and heavy-lidded, widened suddenly and gazed at her with something more than desire glowing in them. Something like sheepishness. "Um . . . pictures?" he managed, his voice still deep and rough.

Limpidly, she said, "I hear you found one

of them. Before we met. Before you rode Jake's roan up the mountain."

"I'm going to kill Ally."

Erin's fingers were still touching his face, trailing along his jaw and tracing his features with seeming idleness. Reproachfully, she said, "And you *said* you came all that way to rescue a writer in distress!"

Matt cleared his throat again. Not that it helped. "And what was I supposed to say? That I fell in love with a picture? You would have shot me!"

If Erin's fingers quivered at that declaration, she at least managed to keep her expression calm. "Big, tough businessman like you?" she mocked softly. "Falling for a picture? I'm afraid I find that hard to believe."

His eyes were growing more heavy-lidded and his hand, which lay on the back of the couch, was tense. But Matt still didn't touch her. "I . . . don't blame you," he said hoarsely. "I didn't believe it myself. I thought I was losing my mind."

Thoughtful, she said, "I imagine a man like you — who understands women so well — is constantly in demand. You must have . . . gotten your feet wet a few times."

Matt swallowed hard. "Um . . . yes. Well, of course. I'm thirty-five, after all."

"After all," she agreed gravely.

"And I *like* women. As companions, I mean." Matt cleared his throat yet again and wondered if she even realized how dizzy he was . . . "I happen to be glad somebody decided there should be — two sexes."

"It makes life interesting. To say the least."

"Erin —"

"You're being very good at keeping your hands to yourself," she noted approvingly.

The heavy lids lifted for an instant as Matt glared at her. "Dammit, Erin —"

"Wonderfully noble." Her voice was gently admiring.

Matt released a sound that Chester would have claimed happily as a lethal growl.

"It would serve you right," she said virtuously, "if I jumped onstage as soon as Stuart sang the first note tomorrow night, and fell into his arms."

There were, Matt thought, things beyond bearing. There were limits past which a man could hardly be expected to control his baser instincts. Especially when a vixen pushed remorselessly past those limits.

He lunged.

Laughing, Erin found herself lying back against the comfortable arm of the couch with her arms happily up around Matt's neck.

"Witch!" he said feelingly.

"We have to see if I can wake in your arms and not pull away," she countered reasonably, laughter fading as her own eyes grew sleepy with desire. She absorbed the heavy weight of him as he lay half on her, her fingers tangling in the silky thickness of his hair, and her limbs felt suddenly heavy. How wonderful, she thought, to be able to feel like this.

"Did you set out to torture me?" he asked gruffly, his lips feathering along her jaw. Then answered himself. "Of course you did!"

"You told me I had to fight for what I wanted," she reminded him throatily, tilting her head back as he began exploring the V neckline of her blouse. His rueful laugh tickled her flesh and made her shiver.

"Honey, you didn't have to bring out the big guns. You can have anything on this earth I can give you."

Erin waited until he lifted his head. She gazed gravely into his taut face and flaring eyes. "I asked for time and you gave me that. I asked for understanding and you gave me that. What I need from you right now . . ."

"Is what?" He kissed her very gently, clearly holding passion rigidly in check.

She pushed a lock of raven hair off his

forehead and smiled slowly. "What I need . . . is balance. You've been giving, Matt, and getting nothing. Let me give."

After a moment he asked very quietly, "What do you want to give?"

Her smile grew, green eyes very bright. "What do you most want from me?"

Matt hesitated, then sighed a bit raggedly. "Your love."

"Then that's what I want to give you."

"Erin —"

"I love you, Matt. I've known it for a long time. I was just afraid to believe it. Afraid I'd created another prince because I was afraid of reality. Afraid you'd go away when I touched you."

"And you aren't . . . afraid of that anymore?" His voice was unsteady.

"I'm not afraid. You're real. And when I touch you, you're still real. And I still love you."

Matt framed her face with shaking hands. "I fell in love with a picture," he said softly. "And then with a prickly rose." He drew a deep breath. "God, Erin, I love you! I've been going out of my mind all week, afraid you'd decide you didn't want me. And when I called this afternoon — you sounded so distant. After I hung up, it was like a kick in the stomach to realize that I'd asked you to come here — within miles of Travis. So damned close to him and to that year you spent with him. I had to come. I had to get here as fast as I could."

"It's just a year now," she said quietly. "A part of my past like any other year. It doesn't matter anymore. He doesn't matter anymore."

Matt kissed her, his lips warm and hard, and Erin instantly took fire, fighting the reins he held on his desire. She fought willfully, even though a small and rueful part of her mind reminded her of just where they were. She didn't listen.

Her arms wound more tightly around his neck, her mouth opening to him, her body straining to be closer to him than was possible. She could feel the thud of his heart against her, feel the runaway pounding of her own heart.

He tore his lips from hers at last, but only so that he could explore the silky flesh of her throat. "Oh, hell, Erin," he groaned. "My sister's house . . . and kids upstairs . . ."

"I know," she murmured achingly. "I have lousy timing. But I love you so much . . ."

Matt groaned again, his hands slipping down to unsteadily open the buttons of her blouse. His mouth trailed hotly down from her throat, lingering in the valley between her breasts. The front fastening of her bra yielded to his touch, and the flimsy lace confection fell away.

Erin gasped, biting her bottom lip when she felt the pull of his mouth, the erotic caress of a swirling tongue. She could feel her flesh swelling at his touch, and a hot, restless emptiness grew in her. She held his head, her fingers locked in his hair, fighting herself now. Fighting a fire burning out of control.

"Matt ..."

His lips found hers again, kissing her so swiftly that she gave him his name with her breath, the aching sound passing from her to him. The duel of their tongues was hot, hungry, desperate with a primitive need denied too long.

Matt tore his lips from hers abruptly, burying his face between her breasts, breathing as if he had just run a marathon. "Erin ... dear God, I want you so much!"

The words were muffled; Erin felt as much as heard them, and she held him as hard as he held her. "We could . . . go somewhere," she managed, having to concentrate to produce coherent words.

His laugh was a ghost of sound, and when he lifted his head, she could see the strain. "Don't tempt me."

"But I want to," she said honestly.

"Oh, hell, don't —" He drew a deep breath. "You have to hear him sing. You have to be sure."

Or maybe you *have to be sure,* she thought suddenly. Sure that year no longer stood between them. She could forgive Matt a twinge of doubt; she had certainly placed heavy enough emphasis on it herself.

Accordingly, she nodded with reluctant acceptance. "All right. But the concert won't make a difference, Matt."

Fingers unsteady, Matt started to draw her bra closed again. But his mind and his body were on two different wave lengths. The creamy mounds of her breasts, their tips pointed with the need he had aroused, beckoned to him. And this time he couldn't block the wistful sound in the back of his throat. His head lowered again, hands releasing the lace to find willing flesh.

Erin promptly forgot his determination in sheer, boundless pleasure. Her hands moved over the rippling muscles of his back, kneading the hard flesh beneath his white shirt, entranced by the strength and power of him. She was so involved in her own feelings, so conscious of the fire he could summon with a touch, she all but forgot that Matt still felt the elusive presence of a rival.

But Matt, his body aching and his mind trapped within the steel threads of passion, was too near the edge to fully control ancient instincts. And those primitive, unreasonable feelings tormented him. She loved him . . . she was *his* . . . but another man had touched her first — however shallowly. Another man had been her first lover . . . had made her pregnant . . . And vows *meant* something to her . . .

"Hell!" The explosion was savagely quiet, utterly primitive, and Matt lifted his head to show her glittering eyes for an instant. "*He's* the one who touched you first, a girl with dreams in her eyes and no shadow in her smile! *He* was first —" Whatever words may have followed tangled in his throat, and Matt kissed her fiercely, almost ruthlessly, in a driven, instinctive attempt to wipe away a ghostly touch that had come first.

After the first shocked instant, Erin understood. It wouldn't have mattered to some men, perhaps most men. It mattered to Matt. It mattered to him that there would be memories he could have no part of, memories of a first lover and a first child. With the best will in the world, she could not turn back the clock.

With the best will in the world, she couldn't be a girl again.

Her body responded to his touch, as always, her fire rising to meet his own, but Erin felt a fleeting despair. She could put Stuart behind her . . . but could Matt? Groping desperately for something, anything, she found it at last.

And though they were still lying on his sister's couch in his sister's house with her children asleep upstairs, Erin forgot everything but convincing him.

His mouth was buried in her throat, bruising in its fierce pressure, but Erin held him with all the strength she could find in herself. "Matt," she whispered achingly, "this is something I've felt only with you. His kisses never made me burn. His touch never made me tremble. I was starving . . . starving and never knew it . . . It was someone else he touched, not me. You have my heart, all my heart, all that I am . . ."

Gradually, almost imperceptibly, the savagery drained from Matt's taut body. His kisses gentled; his caresses were no longer fierce. He took part of his weight off her by rising on his elbows, and carefully fastened her bra and blouse, dropping soft kisses on the creamy flesh before it was covered.

When he finally met her eyes, his own were hot and restless, anxious. "I'm sorry," he murmured finally, his voice deep and husky. "I never thought I'd be jealous — of a memory."

Erin stroked the padded muscle of his shoulders almost compulsively and smiled. "Matt, in every sense except the very technical one, you're my first lover. What you touch in me no one else has ever touched. I love you."

"I love you." He kissed her lingeringly, then shifted them both in a gentle movement until they lay close together, side by side. He held her, resting his cheek against her hair. His body still ached and pulsed relentlessly, but something even wilder had been tamed, and Matt thought he could handle the need for her.

Quietly, he said, "I'm not going up to that empty bed. I think we'll find out, after all, if you can wake in my arms and not pull away."

"I won't pull away." Erin snuggled even closer, finding that her body fit his as if some fate had decreed it. Her body felt heavy, unsatisfied yet still hovering on the edge; she felt no disappointment. Just contentment and a glorious certainty that she had found her match, her mate.

"I wouldn't be able to run from you," she added softly, utter certainty in her voice. "I wouldn't get over you. I'd carry you with me

all the days of my life. If you left me tonight
... or tomorrow ... or years from now ... it
wouldn't matter."

His arms tightened around her. "I need
you, Erin," he said equally softly. "I'm not
whole without you. You've haunted me
since I first saw that picture. So lovely, and
so wary. I want to make certain no one ever
hurts you again. For good or bad — I'm
yours. All of me. There's no part of me you
can't touch. I love you so very much. If I lost
you —" His voice broke, steadied. "If I lost
you, I'd lose myself."

Erin moved her cheek against his
shoulder. "You won't. You won't lose me."

Exhausted both from physical tension
and emotional strain, they both slept deeply.
And held on to each other all night.

Matt woke slowly, instantly aware of her
warmth at his side. He found himself listening instinctively for the even sound of her
breathing, and felt peaceful, some imper-
ceptible tension easing when he heard it.

It was only then that he looked up to find
his sister leaning on the back of the couch
and regarding him with amused eyes. "Old
poker-face," she said in a stage whisper.
"Better put away your cards, old chum.
Every thought shows on your face."

Unwilling to disturb Erin, Matt whispered as well. "Why don't you go away and bother someone else?" he invited politely.

Ally grinned. "We *have* five bedrooms," she reminded him.

"No kidding. With beds and everything?"

"Last time I looked. How come you two didn't end up in one of them?"

"Alison —"

"All right, all right. Breakfast in an hour. You'd better shave." She headed for the kitchen, laughing softly.

Matt remained where he was, for a while at least. He knew that soon the kids would be up, and noisy. The day, with all its distractions and potential problems, was here.

Would she pull away?

He didn't think so. But the subconscious sometimes lays mine fields where one would expect to walk without fear, and Erin had been through a wide range of emotions these last weeks. Perhaps her subconscious was still guarding itself.

He was afraid to put it to the test.

"Good morning," she murmured then, suddenly.

Matt felt himself tense. "Good morning. Ally says breakfast is in an hour."

"I should go and help." Erin raised up on her elbow to smile down at him. Her braid had come loose during the night, leaving the glorious mass free and shining. She was still heavy-eyed with sleep, but no shadows lurked in the green depths of her eyes.

So beautiful it stopped his heart.

And she didn't draw away.

"I love you," he said, whispering because it was the only sound he could manage.

She bent her head to kiss him, a light kiss that rapidly became something else. A little breathless, she said when she could, "I love you, too."

"I suppose," he said, after staring at her for several hungry moments, "we'd better get up."

With a reluctance that both warmed his heart and tested his control, Erin sat up and swung her legs to the floor. "I suppose we'd better."

They met the children in the upstairs hall, noisily deciding who was to have the honor of giving Chester his morning constitutional. The huge dog, sitting patiently between them, gave Erin and Matt a look, but was undisturbed by having his ears pulled as the kids argued.

"Both," Matt said firmly. "Both of you take him."

"But he slept in Danny's room —"

"He likes company," Erin said diplomatically. "I'm sure he'd prefer you both to take him."

With each ear held firmly in a childish hand, Chester lumbered down the hall between them.

Erin and Matt, still laughing, parted company outside their bedroom doors and got their morning decently started with showers and whatnot . . .

They spent the morning at the house, and Erin was both amused and touched to find that Matt was putty in the children's hands. It was clear that his niece and nephew adored him, and equally clear that he returned the affection. He had the rare ability to talk to children without talking down to them, and he was clearly unable to resist whatever blandishments they chose to aim his way.

"He'd give them the earth," Ally told Erin dryly, "if he could. The man's a born father."

Erin offered only a smile to the bright blue gaze turned her way, and Ally sighed gustily. "Well, I have eyes, don't I?" she demanded aggrievedly.

It would have been too much to expect, Erin acknowledged ruefully, that she and Matt could keep their feelings to themselves. They never strayed more than ten feet away from each other all morning, and both the smiles and touches they exchanged, however casual they *thought* they were, would probably have been obvious to a blind man.

They left just before lunch, Matt telling his sister and brother-in-law that they'd be late in returning. He steered Erin determinedly to the family car, saying only that his rental car was a Mercedes with bucket seats.

Smiling, Erin had already moved across the seat to his side by the time he got in.

They did indeed lose themselves in the city — walking, window shopping, talking casually. They had lunch in a small restaurant, and the casual talk dropped away from them. Every meeting of eyes grew more intense than the last, and words that weren't at all casual emerged as husky sounds.

"Erin . . . could you move to New York?"

"As long as you're there," she answered simply.

He drew a sharp breath. "And your aerie?"

She smiled. "It'll always be there. For vacations. Visits from time to time."

"There are demands on me," he warned reluctantly. "Business demands. Sometimes

— late nights. Trips I have to take."

Erin was thoughtful. "I'll cope, Matt. If you want me with you, I'll be there. You won't ask more of me than I'll be able to give."

"Just — tell me if I do. I won't mind so much to know you're waiting, but if you feel stifled and leave —"

She looked at him, realizing suddenly that he wouldn't ask. Matt was so apprehensive of asking too much of her that he was unwilling to ask for a binding commitment. Too conscious that another man had taken constantly from her, Matt was determined to take only what she would give him.

Erin reached across the table to lay her hand over his. "Marry me," she said softly.

Something leaped in his eyes, but Matt cleared his throat before speaking. "If you ever felt trapped," he said roughly, "or had to break your vows, I don't think I could stand it. I *know* that what I feel for you is forever, but —"

"But what?" She smiled gently. "But I may not be sure? I love you, Matt. And what I feel *is* forever. Marry me."

He carried her hand to his lips, his eyes very bright. "Just say when," he murmured.

Erin laughed aloud. "When!"

The audience was restless, thousands of

voices blending into constant sound, a quivering roar. Eyes turned constantly to the curtained stage and the indications of movement behind the concealing draperies.

Erin and Matt, sitting in the center of the third row, waited like the rest for the concert to begin.

"You told him we'd be here?"

She nodded. "If you want to meet him — afterward — we can go to his hotel."

Matt hadn't made up his mind on that point. "We can decide that later," he said, holding her hand firmly.

"All right."

He looked at her, still somehow anxious. If he lost her now — lost her to a prince whose glitter he could never hope to equal — Matt knew he'd go out of his mind.

He thought of minds, of subconscious desires and wishes.

Dammit! Dammit, stop thinking! he ordered.

Instead, he gazed at her. So lovely. So terribly, vitally important to him. She was far calmer than he, her breathing steady, face composed. Her hand was warm and still, no tremors betraying a disturbance of any kind.

She turned her head and smiled at him, and Matt, reassured, lifted her hand briefly to his lips.

What would his life be like without that smile?

It didn't bear thinking of.

The lights dimmed and thousands of voices were suddenly muted, then fell to silence. With the harsh suddenness of a blow, an announcer's voice blared out over the speakers, thundering an introduction no one listened to. The curtain swept back, revealing instruments, cables tangled from amplifiers to instruments, musicians . . . and a lone man in the center of the stage.

The crowd went wild.

Matt realized instantly what Erin had meant by calling Stuart Travis something larger than life. His charm was a palpable, almost visible thing as he talked and joked with the audience, his voice warm and deep. Disdaining the glittering or deliberately sloppy dress of some of his contemporaries, he wore dark slacks and a light open-throated shirt; his dark hair was cut casually and he was clean-shaven. He neither wandered restlessly all over the stage nor moved jerkily, but stood at ease and comfortable in the spotlight.

And then he sang.

He sang to Erin.

He came to the edge of the stage, unerringly finding the warm glow of her hair in the third row; the stage-lights spilled out over several rows. They were close enough to see him clearly, and it was obvious that he saw them.

After a flickering glance, Stuart Travis ignored Matt as though he were an unimportant part of the faceless audience. He gazed only at Erin, sang only to her.

And it didn't take Matt more than the length of one song to realize that Travis was still trying to win his ex-wife back. The first song was about a man falling in love with a woman with hair the color of a sunset. The second song was about a wedding. The third, about a fight — and making up afterward. The fourth, about a peach nightgown and a lovely sleeping face.

It was a strange, stomach-jarring shock for Matt to realize what was happening. He heard the man singing with passion and power and longing. Heard a voice that was incredible in its surging emotions.

Heard a man making love to Erin with music.

And Matt wondered — even he wondered — how Erin could possibly resist the passion and pain and longing in his voice. How any woman could.

He fought the urge to turn and gaze at her profile, taking what comfort he could from the fact that her hand was still warm and steady in his grasp. But he was, in a sense, helpless to fight Travis now. He couldn't fight with the same weapons. He couldn't claim a year of Erin's life — much less remind her of it in such a strong, revealing way.

Even though Matt believed Stuart Travis had never felt the depth of emotion between himself and Erin, he nonetheless heard it in Travis's voice, in his songs.

Then, catching a second flickering glance from the man onstage, Matt realized something else. Travis was attempting a double blow. He was deliberately, mockingly flaunting his entire relationship with Erin beneath Matt's nose — and reminding her passionately of every day they'd spent together. And every night.

Matt kept himself still by sheer willpower, staring at the singer, dimly aware that if eyes had been knives, Travis would have lost his life.

The singer sang, on and on, songs of his life with Erin. And she hadn't exaggerated, Matt thought. Every facet of their life together had been set to music.

Even the loss of a baby.

Matt tightened his hold on her hand as he heard that song, appalled that the man could have been so callous — and so hypo-critical. To Erin he had shown no regret, no grief; to the world he could show both.

From Erin, Matt could feel no reaction at all. He glanced at her profile quickly, seeing only a calm and detached interest, and some of his own tension drained away. That was when he felt her squeeze his hand gently, and he realized that she was very aware of his reaction to all this.

Travis kept singing. Song by song, the passion and appeal in his voice grew stronger, his lean face more intent, his gestures more controlled.

Finally, as the crowd was wildly ap-plauding a song about the painful end of a marriage, Travis smiled a curious twisted smile. He looked directly at Matt for the first time, a long and steady look. Then he saluted the other man in a gesture that seemed to mock both of them.

And sang a last song. A song about an ex-wife's unexpected visit . . . and a very final ending. There was, it seemed, another man. A man who knew how to summon fire, and hold it. A man who had found a woman's love.

Then the stage went abruptly dark, the last echoes of the song ringing out in the blackness of despair.

The crowd went crazy, and was still wildly applauding when the houselights came up. There was no curtain call; Stuart Travis never returned to the stage to accept accolades. The curtains remained closed.

As the rest of the crowd began to rise, Matt did also, almost afraid to look at Erin. She stood at his side, her hand still within his grasp, and said nothing.

Matt nerved himself and looked at her.

She was smiling. "He's very talented. I'd forgotten. And that last bit, killing the lights like that, was very effective, don't you think?"

Matt drew a deep breath. "Very effective. The hair on the back of my neck stood up."

She laughed a little. "Another award winner, that song."

The crowd was moving, surging toward exits, and they had no choice but to move along with the tide. There was no time and no privacy to say what needed to be said, so they were silent. It took nearly half an hour to get out of the building and find their car in the lot.

They sat in the car and watched the tangle of vehicles that would take at least an hour to clear out, and Matt made no effort to join the rush to leave. He talked very quietly, in a voice that was conversational with an effort.

"I knew he was talented . . . but not like that. I listened to him and — I told myself he wouldn't get you back. I told myself you knew him too well now to be fooled by his songs. But I was so afraid he'd win."

Utterly calm, Erin said, "There was never a chance of that."

In the brightness of the parking lot, with the headlights of passing cars flashing from time to time, he could see her very clearly. She looked completely calm. Then she met his gaze and smiled, and he felt his heart lurch at the love he saw.

"Never a chance," she repeated. "Matt, I knew what he was trying to do. And I didn't feel a thing. Oh, I admired his talent, but that was all."

"You're . . . sure?" he asked softly.

"Completely sure." She turned, sliding her arms around his neck, smiling. "I love you, Matt."

Matt drew her even closer and kissed her, his heart pounding, only then realizing how tense he had been, how troubled. Even knowing the shallowness and selfishness beneath Stuart Travis's extraordinary talent, Matt had felt the incredible pull of emotions the other man had flung at them.

And he felt humbled, suddenly, that this woman had chosen him over that other man. It was not a rational thought; he knew that Erin had found in himself qualities Travis could never lay claim to, qualities she needed. But there was an instinctive part of him that was triumphant, as one male always is when he defeats another male.

"I love you," he whispered when he could, drinking in the glow of her green eyes, the tender smile.

"I've nothing at all against your sister and brother-in-law," Erin murmured, "but do we have to go back to their house?" With direct and husky honesty, she added, "I don't want to wait anymore, Matt."

Chapter Nine

He felt as nervous as a sixteen-year-old.

Matt hung up the phone after offering a somewhat incoherent explanation to Ally, then sat and counted to ten silently as he tried to slow his runaway pulse. It didn't work. He stared at the bathroom door and listened to the shower. That didn't help his pulse either.

Rising from the bed where he'd been sitting, he paced slowly over to the window and stared out. They had found this hotel and checked in, with Erin grinning a little at their lack of baggage; Matt had arrogantly stared down the politely surprised desk clerk, resisting an urge to sign the register in the name of Mr. and Mrs. Smith.

It was ridiculous, of course, but he'd found himself forced to deal with several peculiar thoughts and urges since meeting Erin. He had never thought much about conventions of behavior — until now. Modern morals being what they were, he was even vaguely surprised that the desk clerk had looked surprised.

He couldn't help but be amused by himself, realizing that being in love had changed him in many ways. He found himself caring more about conventions, about the opinions of others. Not for himself — but for Erin. He wanted nothing, absolutely nothing, to tarnish their feelings for each other.

He wanted her to have nothing to regret.

He knew that neither of them would regret this night.

Restless, Matt took off his jacket and tossed it over a chair, hardly noticing the bright furnishings of the room. He stood for a moment, staring at that other door, then started toward it, shedding clothing erratically.

The bathroom was steamy, the mirror fogged. Behind the opaque shower curtain, he could barely make out the shape of her body. Hesitating only momentarily, Matt pulled the curtain aside and stepped into the hot, wet enclosure.

She turned, her arms lifted as she thrust fingers through the heavy mass of her wet hair, and smiled slowly. "What took you so long?"

For a moment Matt could only stare at her. His gaze moved slowly over her lovely face, lingering to watch droplets of water trickle gently down the slope of her firm, full breasts. His eyes traced the narrow width of her rib cage, the tiny waist, rounded hips, and long legs, all creamy white and utterly beautiful.

His gaze returned slowly to her face, meeting green eyes that were deep and dark. With infinite restraint his hands lifted to her waist, the touch of her wet flesh a physical shock he could feel down to his bones. He drew her slowly closer, feeling her hands resting lightly on his shoulders, his eyes intent on the droplets of water clinging to her lips.

He bent his head, his mouth touching hers very lightly, tongue searching out the glittering drops of water. He felt her breasts touch his chest, two points of fire branding him, and a harsh sound found its way from the depths of his chest and lost itself in her mouth.

His hands were stroking her body compulsively, learning the shape of her with an unsteady touch. He could feel the fire in her, the response that was instant and total rising up to meet his desire like a wall of flame.

Holding her slippery body, he trailed his lips down her throat, tasting the clean wetness of her flesh. He felt her fingers lock suddenly in his hair as his mouth found a hard nipple, and felt more than heard her gasp. Her head fell back, causing the shower spray to sprinkle over them both.

Matt hardly noticed. Senses starved for the touch of her could hardly be sated now; he couldn't get enough of her. One hand slid down to the small of her back, pulling her lower body hard against his until they were almost as close as they could be.

Almost.

Sanity reared a reluctant head then, and he realized their need was too frantic to allow for athletic contortions in the shower. He turned off the shower blindly and swept back the curtain, keeping an arm around her, reaching for towels.

It took an agony of patience to delay long enough to dry each other in hurried silence and every instant his eyes met hers seemed to stop his heart. He flung the towels aside and gathered her up, lifting her into his arms and carrying her through to the bedroom.

Seconds later, the covers of the wide bed thrown back, Matt gazed down on her lovely face and groaned softly. "Erin . . . my God, you're so beautiful . . ."

Her lips parted beneath his, jade eyes only half open as they looked into his own. Her hands molded his shoulders, traced his spine slowly. One silken leg moved to brush his hip in a smooth, tingling caress.

He lifted his head at last, breathing harshly, their gazes locked. He felt one of her hands slide over his chest, the other along his ribs. Her lips were swollen, beautifully red, her breasts rising and falling quickly. She was looking at him, he thought dimly, as if he were everything she had ever wanted out of life.

"Matt ..."

He reached desperately for some kind of control, a part of him strongly aware of the need to take all the time they could master. His hands moved to shape rounded flesh, his mouth surrounding the hard, throbbing tip of her breast. His own body demanded, pushing recklessly for satisfaction, but Matt found a thread of control and hung on fiercely.

He traced the valley between her breasts with his lips, moving slowly downward over the quivering flesh of her stomach. His tongue dipped hotly into her navel, and he felt a stronger quiver, heard a faint sound from her. He slid his hands along her long legs, rubbing slowly over the satiny skin, moving back up along her hips and under them. He kissed the sensitive hollows above each leg.

He could feel the restless heat of her, and

murmured something low in his throat soothingly, his fingers seeking the slick, hot center of her desire. Erin moaned softly when he found it, her body twisting in a sudden helpless reaction.

She could feel his lips touching her thighs, caressing, moving ever closer to the tormenting fingers. Her legs trembled and there was a molten heat in the pit of her belly, burning her. She wanted to scream, to cry out some wild cry of need and pleasure and agony. And she did cry out softly when she felt his lips touch the ache. She cried out wordlessly, her nerves splintering, all her breath leaving her for an instant in a gasp.

She felt as if she were stretched tightly, about to break, her heart pounding against her ribs with thuds she could feel strongly. All her consciousness seemed to focus on him, on what he was doing to her, and if she could have found words, she would have asked him why he was doing this, why he was tormenting her this way.

But she could find no voice, no words, and the plea in her mind was a desperate, growing agony. She didn't think she could stand it; her entire body rebelled against the torture, twisting restlessly, and her heart was choking her.

He moved, finally, rising above her with a

taut face and blazing eyes, every muscle rigid and quivering. He hesitated, gazing down into her awakened, striving face, seeing the tense desperation there, seeing the jade fire in her eyes.

His own control broke into splinters and his body joined hers in a sudden thrust. Erin cried out, her eyes widening, conscious of nothing but the sheer pleasure of him deep within her. There was an emptiness now filled, and the ache in her was partially satisfied. She cradled his body, her limbs moving to enclose him, feeling the strength and power of him, feeling their hearts pounding together.

There was no time for gentleness, no desire for it. From the first instant they were matched, their bodies moving instantly into a savage rhythm. Tension built strongly, winding tighter and tighter, hot and powerful.

Erin could feel her body reaching, stretching mindlessly for something almost beyond her grasp. But it was there and she knew it, knew somehow that Matt could take her somewhere she'd never been before, somewhere glorious. And she clung to him, murmuring a plea she didn't hear, the emptiness in her filling . . . filling . . . bursting suddenly in a splintering explosion of sensations beyond pleasure. Her entire body shook, heat searing her, and her cry was a breathless sound of exaltation.

Matt groaned harshly when her body contracted around him, his own body surging toward release. He buried himself in her, the white-hot strain of his need giving way suddenly in a burst of sheer ecstasy . . .

She wouldn't let him leave her, her arms tightening mutely when he would have. He kissed the hot flushed skin of her breasts and shoulders, looking at last into her wondering eyes. She was smiling when he kissed her lips, her hands moving over his shoulders slowly, smoothing his damp flesh.

"I love you," he murmured huskily.

Erin traced his lips with a finger that wasn't quite steady. "I love you, too, Matt . . . so much."

He kissed her again, then lifted his head, his eyes flickering with surprise. Erin felt the stirring within her, the renewal of passion, and her body responded instantly.

Matt caught his breath, his eyes half-closing in pleasure. He moved only to gently torment the hard buds of her breasts, his lips and tongue languidly caressing.

Erin locked her fingers in his hair, a soft, kittenlike sound of pleasure escaping her lips. She could feel the slow throbbing within her, feel her body catch the rhythm of it, match it. Tense, she held herself still, eyes closed, breathing shallowly. It was, this time, a soft, slow building of need, a gradual rising of heat.

Tremors shook them both, rhythmic tremors growing in intensity until they gasped suddenly with one breath, bodies straining together for an endless moment before relaxing, going limp, and sated . . .

Erin thought that Matt must have turned out the bedside lamp and drawn the covers up around them; she didn't think she had but couldn't remember. She knew only that she had never before slept so deeply and peacefully.

She woke in the gray dawn hours, aware that her body had prodded her, hungry for these new and wonderful sensations. Matt was awake, stroking her body gently, familiar now with all her most sensitive spots. Drowsy and willing, Erin responded instantly to his touch. She accepted him with natural grace, cradling him, holding him. Moving with him in a gentle, steady rhythm that quickened only gradually until the tension grabbed them sharply and flung them upward in a surge of delight that left them clinging wordlessly to each other.

When Erin woke again, it was late in the morning. She lay in contentment for a while, her head on Matt's shoulder and his arms around her. Stirring finally, she carefully eased herself from his embrace and slid from the bed. He murmured something and turned his face into her pillow, and she smiled a little.

She found his discarded shirt on the floor near the bathroom and picked it up, shrugging into it. A few moments later she spoke softly into the telephone, ordering breakfast for them. Matt slept on.

But he woke with a start when a loud knocking sounded at their door sometime later. He sat up abruptly, blinking.

"Am I decent?" Erin asked him, looking down at herself wearing only his shirt.

Matt took a long look, the sight very effectively waking him up, and said simply, "No."

She giggled.

"You are not," he said, "going to the door in nothing but my shirt. Hang on a minute," he added in a much louder voice directed at the door. He slid from the bed, reaching for discarded clothing. "Who is that?" he asked, nodding toward their visitor.

"Room service. I was hungry." She sat on

the bed and drew her legs up to sit like a Buddha.

Matt straightened, dressed now in his trousers, and gazed down at her for a considering moment. Then he sighed, bent to flip a corner of the bedspread over her legs, and went to answer the door.

Erin sat, pensive and silent, until Matt had gotten rid of the waiter. He wheeled the table into the room after shutting the door behind the young man — who hadn't been able to keep his eyes strictly front and center.

"You're dangerous," he told Erin dryly.

She smiled at him, and Matt felt his heart lurch. *I'll never get over this feeling,* he thought, and it was a wonderful thought. He looked at her, sitting so sweetly in the tumbled bed, her glorious hair falling over her shoulders in a shining curtain of copper, and he felt deeply sorry for any man who didn't have an Erin of his own.

Caveman thoughts, those, but he didn't think she'd mind.

After breakfast — eaten in comfort on the bed — Matt announced his intention of remaining in the hotel for a week. At least.

"We don't have any clothes," she reminded him thoughtfully.

"We don't need any."

"People might wonder."

"Let them." Then he frowned a little. "Would that bother you?"

Erin was surprised. "Of course not, darling. We'll pitch a tent in Times Square if you like —" Her offer ended on a gasp as she found herself tackled gently; she was lying flat on her back with Matt smiling down at her.

"That's the first time," he said between kisses, "you've called me darling. We're going to stay here two weeks."

"But, darling —"

"Three weeks."

Erin giggled and abandoned the world.

They did stay in Denver for two weeks — and a rushed two weeks at that. Blood tests and a license took little time, but a gleeful Ally had sent out a call to the Gavin clan and all showed up for the wedding.

Penny swooped all over the city in a small plane trailing a banner behind her that said IT'S ABOUT TIME, MATT! Her dutiful son was ready to go up and chase her down, but Erin, who had yet to meet the Gavin matriarch, only laughed helplessly.

Erin found herself warmly welcomed by Matt's sisters, all of whom resembled one another — and their mother. They were all tall and dark, and all had clearly married for love — love that had endured. An affectionate family, there was no formality and few manners among them, all of them forthright and cheerful.

Penny Gavin turned out to be a slender, dark-haired woman with an infectious grin and the energetic spirit of all her grandchildren combined. She rushed into Ally's house and hugged Erin delightedly, talking a mile a minute and totally ignoring Matt, who was trying to find out where she'd hidden her plane.

"— and it's going to be just *wonderful* to have you in the family! Good for Matt, you know —"

"Where is it, Mother?"

"— and a redhead! Such lovely hair —"

"Steve, did you see the plane when you picked her up?"

"But I didn't pick her up, Matt —"

"— and I hope you mean to teach him some manners, Erin, because *I* certainly never could —"

"Mother —"

"— interrupting people in the middle of their sentences —"

"Mother, where's the plane?"

Danny came into the room, his large eyes taking in the sight of his favorite uncle.

"Uncle Matt, there are two police cars down the street."

"Well, what's happened?"

"I don't know. Unless," he added thoughtfully, "it's grandmother's plane."

"*What?*"

Danny nodded. "She landed in front of Timmy's house —"

"Oh, for gods —"

"Don't fuss, Matt," Penny begged sweetly, and took the arm of a laughing Erin to lead her away. "He fusses so, my dear. You'll have to teach him better —"

"*Mother!*"

With such a beginning, it was hardly surprising that Erin was nearly breathless with laughter by the time they finally got to church. Her own parents had arrived and fit in very well with the Gavins, accepting Penny's talk of altitude and wind velocity without a blink and clearly pleased with Erin's choice of husband.

The ceremony itself was beautiful and grave, both Erin and Matt conscious of the vows they exchanged and of the strong support of their families.

Erin had left the choice of location for a honeymoon to Matt, and was a little curious as to where they'd go. She was even more curious when the whole family escorted them to the small airport near Steve and Ally's home, and laughed helplessly when they were put solemnly aboard Sadie and Steve climbed gravely into the cockpit.

"Where are we going?" Erin asked her husband, having to nearly shout.

He put an arm around her and grinned, but refused to answer. Bemused, Erin watched the miles fall away from the helicopter, knowing only that they weren't going back to her cabin. They swooped away to the southwest, ending up some considerable time later, and after a stop to refuel, on an island off the coast of California.

It was a small island with a golden beach — and a single neat cottage shaded by tall palm trees.

Erin was wordless when Sadie landed and they climbed out. She stood gazing around her, delight growing, while Matt and Steve transferred bags into the cottage. When Steve and his trusty steed had disappeared into the distance — blaring Ravel for the first time during the trip — she turned to Matt with an incredulous smile.

"Matt . . . it's beautiful!"

He smiled, leading her into the cottage and watching her look around at the comfortable furnishings. "I thought you'd like it.

It belongs to a friend of mine — loaned to us for as long as we like."

"I'll never get my book finished," she murmured, going into his arms.

"Your publisher," Matt said graciously, "has decided to postpone your deadline. Indefinitely."

"He's *such* a nice man. I must buy him a tie or something for Christmas."

"I can think of things he'd rather have."

"Oh? What, for instance?"

"A little . . . TLC. For the man who has everything."

Erin smiled slowly. "Well, that's fine — except that all my tender loving care is spoken for."

"Oh?"

"Mmm. My husband, you know."

"Lucky so-and-so."

Erin kissed his chin. "No, I'm the lucky one. I came home one day and found him sitting on my doorstep, and I was angry. I told him to go away. But thanks to whatever fates were watching over us, he didn't go."

"He was stubborn?"

"Wonderfully stubborn."

He kissed her, then said in a conversational tone, "Do you know that my toes still curl when you smile at me?"

She bit the inside of her cheek. "Um . . .

really? Is that why you looked so peculiar at the altar?"

"Well, it's an odd reaction to have while committing one's life to someone. I mean — honestly. You'd think a grown man could control his toes."

She choked. "Yes. You'd think."

"And his urges." Matt began unfastening the buttons of her blouse, frowning in concentration. "But . . . somehow . . . I can't seem to do it."

"I can't imagine why," she responded solemnly, her own hands busy with his pants. "It's not at all civilized, you know."

"Yes, but what can I do about it?"

"I suppose" — Erin caught her breath as warm lips found her throat — "you should follow . . . your urges . . ."

"Oh, I agree," he murmured. "I really do."

In the two weeks of being with Matt almost constantly, Erin had discovered a wonderful new world of sheer pleasure. Pleasure in his company, in their conversations, in their laughter.

And in their loving.

Most of all, their loving.

Every time he took her in his arms, she wondered if it could possibly get any better.

And every time, it did. With growing knowledge of each other came growing pleasure, even when it seemed impossible that there were still pleasures to learn.

When Matt carried her to the bed in their honeymoon cottage, Erin wondered again if it could . . . possibly . . . get even better.

It could.

And did.

Five years passed. Two little girls — Amanda and Nicole — played in the Gavin house in New York State, with summers spent in the mountains of Colorado. Three more best sellers had been written, the second one completed just as the first stages of another kind of labor began, and the third written in the midst of children's demands in a cheerfully cluttered household.

Six years saw the addition of a son. Lee.

Also two ponies. And a litter of puppies after Chester brought his mate home and she decided to stay. Also a kitten Amanda "found" at a friend's house.

On their tenth anniversary, Matt and Erin returned to the cottage on the little island.

And it just kept getting better.

The employees of Thorndike Press hope you have enjoyed this Large Print book. All our Large Print titles are designed for easy reading, and all our books are made to last. Other Thorndike Press Large Print books are available at your library, through selected bookstores, or directly from us.

For information about titles, please call:

(800) 223-1244
(800) 223-6121

To share your comments, please write:

Publisher
Thorndike Press
P.O. Box 159
Thorndike, Maine 04986